Operation: Forbidden

Operation: Forbidden

LINDSAY McKENNA

First published in Great Britain 2011
by Mills & Boon, an imprint of Harlequin (UK) Limited,
Large Print edition 2011
Eton House, 18-24 Paradise Road,
Richmond, Surrey TW9 1SR

© Lindsay McKenna 2011

ISBN: 978 0 263 22348 4

Harlequin (UK) policy is to use papers that are natural, renewable and recyclable products and made from wood grown in sustainable forests. The logging and manufacturing process conform to the legal environmental regulations of the country of origin.

Printed and bound in Great Britain
by CPI Antony Rowe, Chippenham, Wiltshire

Dear Reader,

The creation and idea for this story comes from my dear friend, Marchiene Reinstra, an Interfaith Minister. Although born in India to Dutch missionary parents, Marchiene lived the first eight years of her life in Pakistan on the Afghanistan border. She has fond memories of that country and its people. It was from her experience and memories about the Afghan people that I developed my hero.

I love Marchiene's perspective on the world. As an Interfaith Minister, she is steeped in many different world religions, including the Muslim faith. Her contention is that all the great religions, while having their fanatics, also have a core group who truly practice what they believe. Marchiene knows quite a bit about the Sufi branch of the Muslim faith. They are the mystics of their faith. She said that the Sufis work from their heart. Everything they do is in praise of God.

My prayers are that one day, all peoples of the world can live in harmony, peace and respect with one another. And with that in mind, please enjoy *Operation: Forbidden*. Let me hear from you at www.lindsaymckenna.com

Warmly,

Lindsay McKenna

As a writer, **Lindsay McKenna** feels that telling a story is a way to share how she sees the world. Love is the greatest healer of all, and the books she creates are parables that underline this belief. Working with flower essences, another gentle healer, she devotes part of her life to the world of nature to help ease people's suffering. She knows that the right words can heal and that creation of a story can be catalytic to a person's life. And in some way she hopes that her books may educate and lift the reader in a positive manner. She can be reached at www.lindsaymckenna.com or www.medicinegarden.com

Chapter 1

Emma was in deep trouble. She'd just signed up for a second tour at Camp Bravo on the front lines of the Afghanistan war. And now this. Her commanding officer, Major Dallas Klein, had just requested her presence. Right now. That couldn't be good. She swallowed hard, and her heart began a slow pound of dread.

"Go on in, Captain Cantrell," the assistant said, gesturing to the C.O.'s office.

Emma nodded, took a deep breath and opened the door. She stepped inside and quietly closed it behind her. "Reporting as ordered, ma'am," Emma said, coming to attention.

Dallas Klein looked up from behind her desk.

"At ease. Have a seat, Captain," Dallas said, pointing to the chair near her desk.

"Yes, ma'am," Emma murmured. Sitting at attention, she clasped her hands and waited. Her boss frowned as she lifted about ten files and put them into her lap. The woman sifted through them, and Emma instinctively knew they had something to do with her. She almost blurted out, *What kind of trouble am I in now?* but didn't. Compressing her lips, Emma held on to her last shred of patience.

"Here it is," Dallas said, opening one file and pushing the others aside. "Captain, you're the only woman in our squadron that speaks Pashto. You took a one-year saturation course before you came over here. Correct?"

"Yes, ma'am." Emma nodded.

"Good. And you continue to use the language?"

"Of course. I get a lot of practice with the Afghans who are allowed to work here on our base."

Dipping her head, Dallas looked down at the thick sheaves of paper in the file. "Very well, Captain. I've just had a highly unusual request dropped on me. And ordinarily, I would tell high command to go stuff it, but this time, I couldn't." Dallas scowled over at Emma. "You really gave your career a black eye last August by rescuing that Special Forces sergeant off a hill under attack. I know Nike Alexander had the idea, but you were the XO at the time, and you implemented her request."

Emma wanted to roll her eyes. God, didn't Klein forget anything? She remained silent; the major wanted her to respond, but what could she say? Yes, she'd screwed up, but she'd also saved a life. Emma knew when to keep her mouth shut, and she held the major's flat stare. Emma had never confessed to what the major just said. If she had, she would probably have been court-martialed. The better choice was to remain alert but mute.

"Well," Dallas growled, jerking open another paper from the file, "I have a way for you to save your career, Captain Cantrell."

Brows raised, Emma was interested. "Oh?"

"Actually," Dallas said, "the Pentagon chose you because you speak Pashto, the common language here in Afghanistan. And frankly, I'd like to see you distinguish yourself in some way so you can eventually go up for major and make the promotion." Dallas thumped the file with her index fingers. "I believe this is a very good way for you to salvage your army career, Captain Cantrell. I hope you think so, too."

Perking up, Emma leaned forward. "I'm interested."

"I thought you might be." Dallas opened up

the file to another section. "This is a very special mission. What I don't like is that you'll be
out of my squadron for six months. You'll be
part of a team working on a unique Afghan
project known as Operation Book Worm."

Emma almost laughed and struggled to keep a
straight face. "Operation Book Worm? Ma'am?"
Dallas appeared completely serious, not a hint
of a smile or joking demeanor. And God knew,
members of the Black Jaguar Squadron played
tricks on each other all the time. Black humor
was alive and well in this combat squadron. It
kept them all sane. Laughter instead of tears.

"This is not a joke, Captain Cantrell, so wipe
that smirk off your face."

"Yes, ma'am." What the hell was Operation
Book Worm?

"Okay, here's the guts of the mission. You're
being assigned to Captain Khalid Shaheen.
He's the only Afghan currently allowed to fly
the Apache combat helicopter. He's been flying

with another Apache squadron in the Helmand province of southern Afghanistan until this operation went active."

Emma's brow bunched. "An Afghan flying one of our Apaches?" She'd never heard of such a thing. And she was being assigned to this dude?

Dallas held up her hand. "Just sit and listen. I don't want you interrupting me, Captain."

"Yes, ma'am."

"Captain Shaheen is a thirty-year-old Afghan. He's responsible for creating Operation Book Worm."

Emma nodded and said nothing. How was this mission going to help *her* career?

"Captain Shaheen comes from one of the richest families in Afghanistan. He is a Princeton graduate and has a master's degree in electrical engineering. He graduated with honors. The army persuaded him to spend six years with them and he proved ideal flying Apache helicopters. The Pentagon is relying on Captain Shaheen to persuade other Afghan military men to come to the United States to be trained at Fort Rucker, Alabama. Once they've earned their wings in Apaches, they will come back to Afghanistan to start fighting and defending their own country."

"Afghanistan does not have an air force."

"No, but Shaheen is the bedrock for starting one."

Emma considered the pilot with new respect. "That's a tall order."

"New ideas start with one person," Dallas said.

"And what is my activity with him?"

"There's more. His sister, Kinah Shaheen, was also educated at Princeton. She's twenty-eight years old and holds a Ph.D. in education. She has made it her mission in this country to provide education to young girls. As you know, under Taliban rule, girls weren't allowed any type of education. Kinah is armed not only with a hell of an education, but her family's money and a fierce determination to get girls back into school."

"Wow," Emma said, "that's an even taller order. I've been here long enough to see how women are suppressed when it comes to education. In the past, the Taliban killed teachers and tribal elders or chieftains of villages who allowed girls to be schooled."

"I know," Dallas said, grimness in her tone. "Kinah and her brother, Khalid, came up with the idea for Operation Book Worm. Khalid is considered a used-car salesman of sorts." She grinned a little.

"You've met him?" Emma was now completely taken by the Afghan brother and sister and their plans.

"Once," Dallas said dryly. "And I can see why Khalid has been able to talk corporations in the United States into donating millions of dollars for this idea. Kinah is no small-time operator, either. Their father is a Persian rug salesman, so talking people out of money is in their DNA."

"But their idea sounds more than saleable," Emma said, excited.

"It has been." Dallas leaned back in her chair. "Between them, they've got ten million dollars to throw at this operation."

"Wow…"

"Yeah, double wow," Dallas agreed. "You'll come into this by virtue of the fact that Khalid is going to use, with the U.S. Army's permission, a CH-47 transport from Camp Bravo. He's qualified in four types of helicopters, by the way. And that's no small feat, either."

Eyes widening, Emma considered that skill. "He must be…"

"He's a genius," Dallas said. "Brilliant, mad and passionate, not to mention a damned fine combat helicopter pilot."

Emma took a deep breath. "He sounds like a Renaissance man. Many skills and talents."

"Oh, Khalid is all of that," Dallas said.

"Why does he need me?"

"He wants to land in each targeted village not only to deliver books, supplies and food, but to show you as an example of what a woman can do. Khalid wants the girls of the village to see a woman who flies that helicopter. He feels that show-and-tell is a quick way to get the girls to dream big and often."

"That's a great strategy," Emma said, understanding the Afghan's brilliant concept. "So, I'm his copilot?"

"You're both aircraft commanders—ACs. You're the same rank. You have three years less time in the Apache than he does, but he wants you in the driver's seat off and on."

"In other words, he has a live-and-let-live policy about swapping out AC status?"

"Yep. You'll find Khalid one of the most fascinating men you've ever met. He'll keep you on your toes. He wanted a woman Apache pilot who spoke Pashto because he wants that woman to be able to speak to the little girls. He wants you to become a saleswoman to encourage their education. And don't be surprised if he has you do impromptu speeches on why little girls should want an education. Khalid wants to fire their imaginations. He wants to shock them from the realm of dreams to that of possibilities."

"I'll be happy to take on this mission, ma'am," Emma said.

"For the next six months, from spring through fall, you'll work with him. He plans on having fifty schools set up along the border villages by the time snow flies."

"But," Emma said, holding up her hand, "haven't you left out one thing? You know all the border villages are wide open to attack from the Taliban? Those villagers live in fear of them. And how does Khalid protect all these villages? Once the Taliban hears of schools for girls, you know they'll attack and kill the teachers."

Dallas nodded grimly. "He's very well aware of the situation, and the U.S. Army is coordinating with him to protect these villages. They'll be moving more Special Forces A-teams *into* the villages. And air force drones will be utilized as flyovers on a nightly basis by our CIA guys stationed here when the Taliban is active. This could be a queen-maker for you, Captain Cantrell."

Emma considered the assignment carefully. If she could successfully work with Captain Shaheen and his sister, her personnel jacket would contain glowing commendations from them. Enough to bury the censure over her decision last year. And then her family, who had a nearly unbroken ribbon of service to America, would no longer have this blight on its reputation. As she sat there contemplating all of this, Emma then wondered: could she get along with this Afghan? He was filthy rich. Princeton-educated. Would he look down on her? Not appreciate what she brought to the table with her own intelligence and creativity? Suddenly, Emma felt unsure.

Dallas signed the orders and handed them across the desk to her. "Here you go, Captain Cantrell. Do us proud." She hesitated for a moment and added, "Be warned: He's a marked man. The Taliban has a huge reward out for his death. This is going to be no picnic for you. Captain Shaheen is landing in—" and she looked at her watch "—fifteen minutes. Be on the tarmac to meet him. Dismissed."

The sun was bright and Emma put on her dark aviator glasses. The breeze was inconstant across the concrete revetment area. The odor of flight fuel was strong. She watched as several ordinance teams drove out in specialized trucks, pulling their loads of weaponry on trailers. An excitement hummed through the area. Emma inhaled it and absorbed the vibrating tension. She loved that feeling, which was probably why she was an Apache combat helicopter pilot.

Some anxiety lingered about the new assignment. If Shaheen was a marked man, on the enemy's top-ten-wanted list, it was more than likely the Taliban would make good on their threat to murder him.

Then there was her own distrust of rich men who thought they could act reprehensibly without recourse. Like Brody Parker. Brody had been a rich American in Lima, Peru, and she'd met him when flying in for the original Black Jaguar Squadron. A year after falling helplessly in love with him, Emma found out he was married, with children. Stung to her soul by the lies that men could tell, she'd made a point of avoiding the opposite sex since coming to Camp Bravo. It was a clean start. She didn't need another rich, lying bastard to deal with.

Shaheen landed the Apache on a three-point landing about a hundred feet away from where Emma stood. It was a perfect landing—gentle and not bouncy. Her eyes narrowed as she saw the ground crewman place the ladder against the bird and climb up after the rotors stopped turning. He hefted the canopy upward on the front cockpit after it was unlocked by the pilot. Emma was confused; she saw no pilot in the back seat. No one flew the Apache with just one pilot unless it was an emergency.

When Khalid Shaheen climbed out of the cockpit, he handed the crewman his helmet, and Emma smiled to herself. As the Afghan emerged, she was taken by his lean, taut form. He had to be six feet tall, which was about the top height for an Apache pilot. Most were between five foot seven inches and five foot ten inches tall. The cockpit was cramped, and anyone over six feet couldn't comfortably get into it. She tried to ignore his animallike grace as he climbed out of the cockpit and stood on the dark green and tan metal skirt. The crewman stepped off the ladder and waited nearby.

Emma took in Shaheen's olive skin, military-short black hair and straight, dark brows above narrowed blue eyes. When he smiled and joked with the crewman on the tarmac, her heart suddenly thumped hard in her chest. Shaheen was eye candy, no doubt. And dangerous… His face was narrow, his nose aquiline, cheekbones high and he had a strong chin. When he smiled at a crewman's joke, his teeth were white and even. Emma felt herself melting inwardly. Of all the reactions to have! Shaheen was like a fierce lion moving with a feral grace that took her breath away. There were no lions in Afghanistan, Emma reminded herself.

And yet, she couldn't take her gaze off the

charismatic officer. He removed his Kevlar vest and placed it on the skirt of the Apache. There was a .45 pistol strapped to his waist. Emma decided that if she didn't know he was Afghan, she would never have guessed it. From this distance, he looked like a typical U.S. Army combat pilot.

The crewmen and Khalid joked back and forth, and the three of them stood laughing. Warmth pooled in her chest and Emma unconsciously touched her jacket where her heart lay. There was such gracefulness to this tall, lanky warrior. Emma suddenly felt as if she were standing on quicksand. Her reaction wasn't logical. The pilot walking languidly, like a lordly lion toward her, was married. He had to be. He had to have a wife and children. Afghans married very early. So why was she feeling shaky and unsure of herself? Emma had never had such a powerful emotional reaction to a man. Not ever, and it scared her.

As Emma stepped forward, her mouth went dry. She forced herself to walk confidently out on the revetment and meet the foreign pilot. And when his gaze locked onto hers, she groaned. Shaheen drew closer, and Emma could appreciate the curious color of his eyes. They reminded her of the greenish-blue depths of the ocean around a Caribbean island. Not only that, his eyes were large, well-spaced, with thick lashes that enhanced the black pupils. She felt as if she could lose herself within them. Emma jerked her gaze away. What was going on? Her heart pounded as though she was on an adrenaline rush. But she wasn't in danger. No, this was excitement at some unconscious level within her that she had never experienced. And that made Emma wary.

Shaheen unzipped his olive-green flight suit as he approached. Black hairs peeked out from beneath his dark-green T-shirt. He reached inside his flight suit. And what he drew out made Emma's jaw drop. Shaheen slowed and stopped about three feet in front of her. In his hand was a huge red rose, its petals flattened from being crushed inside his flight suit, but a rose, nevertheless.

Pressing his hand against his heart, Shaheen bowed slightly and murmured the ancient greeting that all people in the Muslim world shared. *"As-salaam alaikum."* Peace to you from my heart to your heart. "Captain Emma Cantrell?" he asked, smiling as he lifted his head.

Paralyzed, Emma stared up at him. Shaheen held the drooping rose toward her. He'd obviously picked it just before the flight and carried it inside his suit to her. Emma could smell the spicy fragrance of the bedraggled flower. "I—yes," she managed in a croak. Without thinking, she took his gift and responded, *"As-salaam alaikum."* She clutched the rose in her right hand, noting that the thorns had been cut off so it would not prick her fingers.

Scrambling inwardly, Emma tried not to be impressed by this thoughtfulness. When she raised her head, she noticed Khalid's masculine smile and twinkling eyes. "I'm Captain Emma Cantrell," she said in a crisp tone. "Welcome to Camp Bravo." God, she sounded like a teenager on her first date, her voice high and squeaky. Worse, he had the same kind of swaggering, super confidence that Brody had had. They could be twins. Her heart sank. *Not this again.*

"Thank you, Emma. Please," he murmured in a low, husky tone, "call me Khalid once we get out of the military environment."

She stood looking helplessly at the rose in her hand. "Why...I never expected this, Captain Shaheen." Officers simply didn't give other officers flowers. Clearly, he was flirting with her.

Khalid's hands relaxed on his hips, a typical aviator stance. "I went out to my rose garden this morning. I live in Kabul. It is the first rose of the season. I took my knife and cut it off knowing that I wanted you to have something beautiful from me to you."

Emma swallowed hard. Aviators never wore jewelry of any kind. Not even a wedding ring. But this guy had to be married. He was just too charming. The confusion must have shown on her face.

"Rumi, the great Sufi mystic poet, said much about the beauty of a rose." He then quoted her a passage that he'd memorized.

Emma was sure now he was flirting with her. Completely stunned by Khalid's warmth, his utter masculinity and those gleaming blue eyes, Emma choked. "But…you're married!" Well, that wasn't exactly polite, was it? No, but the words flew out of her mouth. Emma took a step away from him. Khalid's face was overcome with surprise, his straight, black brows rising. And then he laughed. His laughter was hearty, unfettered and rolled out of his powerful chest.

"I'm afraid I'm not married," Khalid said and he held up his hands, smiling over her mistake.

Emma didn't know what to do. She knew how she felt toward him—as if he were a conquering Afghan warlord who had just swept her off her feet, stolen her young, innocent heart and claimed her. His smile was so engaging her heart appreciated it by beating erratically. Brody Parker had wooed and wowed her the same way. Oh, God, it was the *same* situation all over again!

Emma gripped the red rose until her fingers hurt. Should she give it back to him? Throw it away? This wasn't military protocol between two officers. Emma furtively looked around her. Who had seen him do this? Had they seen her accept the gift? Things like this just weren't done in the U.S. Army. Could she be more distressed?

"I can't take this, Captain Shaheen." She handed him the rose.

Holding up his hands, Khalid said, "Forgive me, Captain Cantrell. My father is Sufi and I was raised with Rumi. I see all of my life through this thirteenth-century poet and mystic's eyes. I am forever quoting him, for Rumi guides my heart and my life. I hope you do not take offense to my gift. Among the Sufis we believe that love is the only vehicle to touch the face of God and become one with the source. My gift to you was merely an acknowledgment, heart-to-heart, that we are connected. And it is a gift that honors you as a person, to show that you are sacred to me and all of life. Please, do not be pained by the gift."

Stubbornly, Emma gave him a long, steady stare. "It's not acceptable military behavior, Captain. Let's leave it at that, shall we?"

Khalid winced. He pressed his hand to his heart and held her gaze. "I will maintain correct military protocol with you, Captain. Please accept my deepest apology. I am honored that you have agreed to work with me." He tucked the rose back into his flight suit.

Emma wasn't sure about this terribly handsome Afghan standing in front of her, speaking with such candor. Her heart melted over the warmth dancing in the depths of his aquamarine eyes. Given the sincerity in his voice and face, she wondered obliquely if she'd read his intentions wrongly.

"Then we're in agreement," she said in a clipped tone. "I volunteered for this mission to help the Afghan girls get an education." Emma tried to convince herself that he was Brody Parker all over again, only even more charming and smooth than her lover in Peru had been. Emma wasn't falling for it again. Her heart couldn't take the hurt twice. Dallas's words haunted her: *This could be a queen-maker for your career.* And more than anything, Emma wanted to get good remarks from Shaheen after she finished the six-month mission. Now, she felt as though she was literally walking the edge of sword that could cut her both ways. What had she just stepped into?

Chapter 2

Emma tensed. A range of emotions passed across Khalid's rugged face. "Look," she murmured, "I know that in different cultures, mistakes can be made."

"No, no," Khalid said, trying to muster a smile, but failing. "You need to understand the heart of our mission. By knowing what the foundation is, you can appreciate our fierce passion for our people." He held her forest-green gaze. The noise on the tarmac surrounded them. He gestured for Emma to follow him into the Ops building where there would be a room where they could talk.

Emma followed Shaheen. More and more, this felt like doom to her. She was falling fast and she needed to focus on her work. Inside Ops, the captain found an empty room. They went in and closed the door. There was a rectangular table, reports scattered across it along with pens. Emma took a seat and he sat down opposite her after pouring them some coffee.

Taking the lead, Emma folded her hands and met his stare. "My CO told me you were a marked man. I want to know what that means since I'm putting my butt on the line here."

"I have an ancient enemy," Khalid began, "his name is Asad Malik. He was born in Pakistan, along the border in the state of Waziristan. Malik was very poor, and with the Taliban, who make a permanent home in that border state, he found his calling. My father's family are Sufis. They know that education is the door to all fulfillment of a person's dreams and goals. My father has considerable wealth, and he poured it into the border villages of our country a long time ago because the so-called central government of Afghanistan ignored them."

Brows drawing downward, Khalid said, "Malik rose to become a very powerful Taliban leader. He is heartless and ruthless. He began attacking villages to which my father was trying to bring schools and education. There were many pitched battles over the years, and Malik swore to kill every member of my family."

Emma gasped. Although she knew revenge ran deep, the admittance was still shocking. "What?"

Shrugging, Khalid said, "Malik is not a Sufi. He is a terrorist at the other end of the Muslim religion. Our beliefs swing from an eye-for-an-eye attitude to one of spiritual connection with Allah." He pressed his hand to his heart. "I am Sufi. Malik is stuck in a state of twisted hatred and revenge. It would not matter what religion he embraced, he would practice what he is, despite it. He has perverted the Koran for his own goals."

Emma nodded. "Yes, every religion has its fanatics. In my year here in Afghanistan, I've lived among the Muslims and I find them incredibly generous and caring. They aren't the terrorists that the world thinks. They believe in peace."

"Yes, we are peaceful," Khalid agreed. "It will only be through our daily life that we show the Muslim religion is not one of terrorism."

"It's a PR game," Emma said. "And I agree with you, people are educated one person at a time. Religion doesn't kill. It's the individuals within any religion who choose to interpret it according to their own darkness and wounds."

He gave her an intense look. "I have truly made the right decision in asking you to be a part of our mission. I like your free-thinking policy."

Emma tried not to be swayed by his compliment and felt heat enter her cheeks. "I try never to judge a person. I let their actions speak louder than their words." The intensity of his gaze made Emma feel as if she were unraveling as a woman—not as an officer—to this lion of a man. She mentally corrected herself once again: there were no lions in Afghanistan. Instead, Emma regarded him as the rare and elusive snow leopard that lived in the rugged mountains of this country.

"My death dance with Malik," Khalid continued, "took on new dimensions two years ago. Malik stalks the border like the wolf that he is. He continually attacks and kills the villagers who try to better their lives in any way. It is how he stops my father's generosity to lift the poor up and help them succeed. Malik does not care about such things." Taking a deep breath,

Khalid continued, his voice strained. "I fell in love with a beautiful teacher. Her name was Najela. I courted her for two years and I asked her to become my wife."

Emma heard Khalid's voice quaver and noticed how he fought unknown emotions, his hands opening and closing around the heavy ceramic mug in front of him. She wanted to reach out and touch him, to soothe away the grief she saw clearly etched in his face. But Emma said nothing. She allowed Khalid to get hold of himself so that he could continue his story.

"Najela and my sister Kinah were the best of friends. And why wouldn't they be? They were both American-educated and trained in education. Najela graduated from Harvard and my sister from Princeton. They were working with my father to help set up village schools for boys and girls. I was away working for the U.S. Army and they were frequently up in this area while I flew Apaches in the southern region of my country."

Emma steeled herself. She leaped ahead and figured out that Najela was dead. At Malik's hands? She hoped not. Her heart cringed inside her chest. "Go on," she urged him, her voice tense.

Nodding, Khalid swallowed hard, took a drink of his coffee, wiped his mouth with the back of his hand and then took a deep breath and released it. "I was on a mission with the U.S. Marines in the south when I got word that Malik had captured Najela in one of the villages." His voice became low and strained. "By the time I was given orders to fly north to the village, Malik had repeatedly raped her and then he…slit her throat. I found her in a mud house that had been abandoned by the family who lived there. All I found…was her…" And he closed his eyes for a moment, reliving that nightmare afternoon.

"I—I'm so sorry," Emma whispered, caught up in his anguish. Without thinking, she reached across the table and touched his hand. And when she realized what she'd done, Emma quickly pulled her hand back. No officer should be seen initiating such an intimate action with another officer. Turning her focus back to Khalid, she thought she saw tears in his blue eyes for just a second. And then, they were gone. Had she imagined them? Emma chastised herself for losing her standards.

"Malik hates anyone and anything who tries to improve upon the villagers' lives," Khalid continued, his voice rough. "As I said, he's sworn vengeance against my family because of my father's generosity to the villagers."

Emma considered his heavily spoken words. "And is Malik out there right now? Will he be our enemy as you and Kinah set up this mission for those same villagers?" A cold chill worked its way up her spine as she saw his expression still and become unreadable.

"Yes, he is our nemesis. You need to know that this mission is dangerous so that you remain on guard. Your CO was correct in telling you I am a marked man. You will be marked too, Captain."

Eyes rounding, Emma sat up. "Aren't you afraid, Captain Shaheen? He's already killed one person you loved. You could be next." Suddenly, Emma wanted nothing to harm this man who had a vision for the girls of his country. She could see his sincerity and the heart that he wore openly on his sleeve. Khalid was priceless in her world because few men could be so in touch with their emotions and share them as he just had with her. Brody had never opened up like this. Not ever. And it threw Emma.

Khalid said, "Rumi would say a real Sufi laughs at death. A Sufi is like an oyster—what strikes it does not harm the pearl within."

Considering the saying from the thirteenth century, Emma grimaced. "Sorry, but I'm not in agreement with Rumi. I don't feel I could be at peace if someone raped and then murdered my fiancée."

"I understand," Khalid said. "You have lived in our country where the threat to your life exists every day." He opened his hand and gestured around the room. "Afghans have been at war with the Russians. Now, we have the Taliban. Do we want to live this way? No. Do we dream of a peaceful life? Yes. I don't expect you, Captain Cantrell, to believe as we do. Najela was Sufi. I know in my heart of hearts that throughout her terrible last hours she felt compassion for Malik. He's a man so filled with hatred and vengeance that I'm sure that her compassion only made him want to harm her even more."

Shaking her head, Emma muttered, "Well, I sure wouldn't be thinking peaceful and loving thoughts if that dude was doing that to me. I'd be looking for any way to protect myself and kill the bastard."

Giving her a slight smile, Khalid nodded. "Sufis are misunderstood even by our other Muslim brethren. In fact, those who choose jihad and become terrorists hate us as much as they do the so-called infidels."

"Which is why Malik hates you?" Emma wondered.

"He hates my family for many reasons and has sworn vengeance against each of us. In part, because we are Sufis and believe in tolerance and generosity toward others. The fact my father is worth billions of dollars makes Malik hate us because he was raised in poverty. He didn't own a pair of shoes until he was eleven years old when the Taliban leader recruited him."

Suddenly, there was a deafening explosion outside. The sound and reverberation slammed into the room. Instantly, they both dove for the deck, hands over their heads. Emma hissed a curse. Tiles from the ceiling fell around them as a second explosion shook Ops.

"It's the Taliban," she growled, getting to her feet. Automatically, she pulled the .45 pistol from her belt and ran to the door. Swinging it open, Ops looked like a beehive that had been overturned.

Shaheen was at her side, looking down at her. Emma's face was set and her gaze aimed at the windows outside. He saw one of the helicopters burning, the black smoke roiling and bubbling skyward. "Do you get attacks often?"

Grimly, Emma moved toward the center of Ops. Pilots and crews were hurrying out the doors, armed and ready to fight. She knew from being here over a year that such attacks were sporadic. "No," she snapped, moving with everyone else toward the doors. "Come on, we need to help the fire crews."

Khalid didn't know Camp Bravo as she did. He trotted across Ops and found himself outside with her. Emma's eyes were searching the end of the runway and she pointed in that direction. "That's one of the places they hit us. They sit in the brush beyond the runway and lob RPGs, rocket propelled grenades, this way."

Khalid noted a squad of Special Forces speeding away in a Humvee, armed and ready for battle. He wanted to protect Emma. It was his natural reaction. Telling himself she was a warrior like him, he kept his thoughts and his hands to himself. She was all business now. Another crew rolled up in a fire engine and began spewing foam over the burning CH-47 transport helicopter, already a total loss.

Emma turned. She was glad she had her Kevlar jacket on because gunshots were suddenly being traded at the end of the runway. "Come on, this is under control. No sense standing out here like targets." She gestured toward Ops again.

Shaheen wasn't so sure, for a minute longer, he watched the Special Forces from the Humvee spraying the bushes where the Taliban had been hiding. "Do they get inside the camp?" he asked as he followed her into Ops.

"Not so far, but we're always watching." Settling the .45 back into the holster on her waist, she added, "We're never safe here. Let's get back to discussing the mission, shall we?" Emma stopped and poured herself another cup of black coffee from the urn at the side of the Ops desk. Khalid did the same and they returned to the meeting room.

There were several enlisted men in there. They'd already picked up the ceiling tiles that had dropped from the explosion, so Emma thanked them and, once more, she and Khalid were alone. They pulled their chairs to the table and sat down. Her heart pounded and she felt tense and on guard. As she sipped the coffee, she hoped it would soothe her jangled nerves.

"Will they attack more than once in a day?" Khalid wondered. He found himself drowning in her dark, forest-green eyes, fraught with care and concern. If he read her correctly, it was concern for his welfare. That touched and warmed his wounded heart. There was something ethereal about Emma. Was it how her mussed red hair curled slightly at her temples? Was it her huge green eyes fraught with compassion? Or those lips that reminded Khalid of a rose in full bloom? His inspiration to cut the first red rose of the year from his family's garden hadn't gone as he'd hoped. "Well, let me lay out some information to you on Operation Book Worm," he said, returning to business.

Asad Malik crept away from the end of the runway with his men. Bullets were singing around them, but he knew from long experience that the Special Forces couldn't see them and they were firing blindly into the thick brush. One day, when there was time, such brush would be cleaned away. He had ten men with him. They continued to work their way through the heavy brush, their AK-47s and grenade launchers in hand. Smiling to himself, he congratulated them in a whisper on destroying one of the helicopters. It was a good day!

Dressed in baggy brown trousers, a crisscross of wide leather straps containing bullets across his chest, Malik did not think this attack was done. No. He would wait, skulk through the brush with his men and wait on the other side. Malik knew this forward base was vital to the war effort by the infidel Americans. Until lately, he'd not had enough money to buy more grenades and bullets. Now, he had a new donor from Saudi Arabia who had given him millions to support the Taliban effort.

Grunting and breathing hard, Malik knelt,

hidden. He waited for his ragtag group of nine other men to catch up with him. Most were barefoot, their clothes thin and threadbare. They were all skinny, their cheeks sunken, for coming here had been hard on them. Malik usually worked other areas, but this base was crucial to the American mission and he'd wanted to strike the head of the snake finally.

"Everyone all right?" he demanded roughly as they sat in a semicircle around him. "No wounds?"

"None, my lord," one of the bearded men spoke up.

Malik grinned. "Good. Now, let's sneak around the other side of the runway. Knowing the infidels, they'll think this attack is over."

There were soft, knowing chuckles from the men, all of whom nodded their accord to follow their charismatic and brave leader.

"Come!" Malik whispered harshly, lifting his

hand and moving forward. "I want another he-licopter," he snickered.

Emma could see the burning intensity in Khalid's blue eyes as they narrowed speculatively upon her. They'd just finished off their coffees and got down to the business at hand. She felt giddy and thrilled with his interest in her. Sure, he respected her as a professional, but she sensed something deeper. Sternly, she chided herself for thinking he was drawn to her.

And then her heart contracted. Was Khalid interested in her or was she imagining things? That couldn't be. Khalid was the head of the mission and held power over her. His comments would eventually go into her career jacket. Maybe he was this charming with everyone. She couldn't allow herself to get involved with this intriguing, romantic Afghan warrior. But why did he have to be so damn good-looking?

She vowed to savor this rugged male pilot secretly; he'd never know it. She could hide her feelings. For now.

Khalid pulled out a map from one long pocket on his flight suit leg and spread it out before them. He stood up and, using a pen, said, "This is the route we're going to follow. We'll move from one village to another." His index finger was on the map, tracing the small villages along the border with Pakistan. It bothered him that he was drawn to Emma, despite her military demeanor. Khalid refused to put another woman in the gunsights of Asad Malik. It would be too easy to become personal with red-haired, brazen Emma Cantrell.

"For the next six months," he said, straightening and moving his shoulders as if to shrug off the tension gathered in them, "you will be with me and Kinah, and you will surely be well-educated into our Sufi world. We believe that all religions have a good message for the spirit. My father, who was born in Kabul, comes from a long line of Sufis. My mother, who is a medical doctor from Ireland, continues to this day to be a Presbyterian missionary. She came to this country after she finished her residency in Dublin, Ireland. Her father is an elder in their tradition. And her entire family has been missionaries here in Afghanistan for nearly a hundred years."

Surprised, Emma's brows rose with that information. "Then…you're half-Afghan and half-Irish?" Maybe that accounted for those dancing blue eyes that always had a bit of devilry lurking in their depths.

"I am," he said with pride. "I am a good example that east meeting west can actually get along."

"Your religions are so different."

"That's what I'm trying to tell you," Khalid said, turning the map over. "The Sufis have no quarrel with any other religion in this world. We accept people as they are and respect their beliefs."

"Too bad that all religions can't hold the same ideas," Emma said. She was thinking of the evil Asad Malik.

"That's why," Khalid explained, "the jihad-ists who are twisted and out of touch with true Muslim traditions, hate Sufis and will kill them on sight. The terrorists among those who profess to be Muslim are threatened by the enlight-ened ways of the Sufi people."

Emma sat back. "And so you have no trouble being half-Christian and half-Muslim?"

Chuckling, Khalid shook his head. He spread a second map on to the table. It showed close-ups of some of the more major villages along the Afghanistan-Pakistan border. "Absolutely none. Sufis honor and respect every religious tradition on the face of our Earth. We believe all paths lead through the heart to the Creator, no matter what name you call him or her."

Emma watched as he traced a red line around certain areas. "What are those?" she demanded.

"This is Malik's territory, where he and the Taliban are constantly attacking the villagers."

Emma got up and leaned over, their heads inches apart as she studied the map. "This guy is big. I know I've heard his name."

"Yes, he's north of your base camp."

Emma straightened. "Like you said, we'll be alert."

"Agreed," Khalid said. He picked up the papers, neatly folded them once more and tucked them away in the leg of his flight suit. "So, Captain Cantrell, are you ready to fly back to Bagram Air Force Base with me? We have much to do and there's so much to show you about our mission."

Surprised, Emma watched as Khalid stood, lean, strong, his broad shoulders thrown back with unconscious pride. "Bagram? I thought we'd be working here, out of Camp Bravo?"

"Oh, we will," Khalid assured her. "I'm inviting you to have dinner with me tonight at my family's villa in Kabul. You may stay overnight. As you know, there are male and female sections to each home. I have had our housekeeper prepare you a room in the women's part of the house. After we have a wonderful dinner, I will take you to my office and show you Operation Book Worm. I think you will appreciate what I'll show you. Then, you can grasp even more of the mission and its priorities."

Shocked by the offer, Emma sat staring up at him. "But…"

"This is a work invitation, Captain Cantrell. I'm an excellent host. It's easier for me to show you what we will be doing at our villa where it is all stored, than to try and lug it piecemeal back and forth to this camp."

Emma considered the unexpected invitation

and her vivid imagination took off. What would it be like to be with this Afghan warrior? And truly, that's what Khalid was. She knew he professed compassion and love for others, but her body was not reacting to him in that way. No, she felt a hunger and drive to know Khalid on a much more personal level. How was she going to keep this fact a secret? Looking deeply into his eyes, Emma realized that this wasn't at all personal to Khalid; it was merely a formality to offer her dinner. After all, Emma knew from experience that all Afghans, rich or poor, would automatically invite her to their home for dinner. It was a custom and way of life in Afghanistan.

"Of course I'll go with you, Captain Shaheen. I look forward to it."

Khalid brightened. "Excellent. If there is anything you need to pack in your flight bag before we take off, why not go get it now. I'll meet you back at Ops."

Good, he was remaining all business. As she walked with Khalid out of Ops and into the warming sunlight over the camp, Emma couldn't explain the happiness threading through her. Khalid bowed slightly where the path forked and led to Ops. The fire had been put out on the destroyed helicopter and there was still a lot of activity on the tarmac.

"I'll see you soon, Captain?"

"Yes," Emma said, "this won't take long." Khalid was all business. All military. That warm smile, those inquiring blue eyes of his were veiled.

"Good, I'll meet you at our Apache." He strode confidently back into Ops to file their flight plan.

Shaking her head, Emma trotted down another dirt avenue between the desert-tan-and-green tents. Khalid and Brody had a lot in common, but she'd never spent too much time with a man who had one foot in the east and one foot in the west. The breeze ruffled her red hair as she continued to jog down the dirt path. Making a left, she found her tent and unzipped it. Worry hovered over her. Above all, she had to keep her silly heart out of this. It was bad enough that Khalid was in the active gun sights of Asad Malik, but the Taliban leader would target her, too. In a heartbeat.

As Emma packed essentials into her canvas flight bag, she couldn't stop thinking about Khalid. He'd loved and lost his bride. That explained why he was still single at thirty, unheard of for a Muslim man. She replayed the grief that was raw and alive in his eyes as he'd shared the tragedy of Najela's death at Malik's hands.

After grabbing her toothbrush, toothpaste, comb and brush, Emma quickly finished her packing. She zipped up her flight bag and took her helmet bag off the makeshift chest of drawers. As she headed outside, she felt the sunlight warming up the coolish temperature. She turned on the heel of her flight boot and walked quickly down between the rows of tents. Despite the unexpected Taliban attack an hour earlier, the air was alive with the puncturing sounds of helicopters landing and taking off once more. The smell of jet fuel was always around. Metallic, oily smoke still hung above the camp from the destroyed chopper. The growl of huge military trucks belching blue smoke, their coughs and grinding of gears, filled the air, too. As she jogged across the camp to the control-tower area, Emma's heart took off.

Why did she feel giddy? Like a school girl who had a crush on the all-star football quarter-back? Would she be able to tread on the edge of the sword with Khalid? Separate out her womanly need to know more about him on a personal level from the professional one? Emma wasn't sure. She slowed to a walk and pulled open the door to Ops. As she moved through the busy building and out the other door to the tarmac, Emma sensed her life was about to change. Forever.

Chapter 3

Emma was surprised that Khalid insisted she be the AC—air commander, on the Apache that was to be flown to Bagram. She stowed her bag in a side slot of the combat helicopter. Mounting the helo, Emma was strapped into the back cockpit in no time. She tried to ignore Khalid's charisma as he climbed into the cockpit in front of her. The sergeant helped her and then tended to Khalid's needs. A sudden shiver of warning went up her spine. The whole base was on high alert because of the attack.

Looking around, lips compressed, Emma saw the remains of charred, still-smoking helicopter that the Taliban had destroyed with a grenade launcher. To her left, several Humvees contained Special Forces who were still looking for the terrorists who committed the offense. Something was wrong....

Malik lay on his belly, the binoculars to his eyes. He studied the Apache combat helicopter, more interested than usual in the pilots. Actually, one pilot. A snarl issued softly from between his full, thick lips. Allah had blessed him! There was his sworn enemy, Khalid Shaheen, in the front seat of the Apache. Mind spinning, Malik watched intently.

So, Shaheen was back in the northern provinces? Malik had his spies and they kept him somewhat updated on his enemy's whereabouts. The last Malik had been told, Khalid was in Helmand Province flying Apaches

against his brothers in the Taliban. Malik knew
where Shaheen lived in Kabul. He and his up-
start, rebellious sister, Kinah, could be found
at their family home from time to time. Was
that where he was going? A hundred questions
ranged through Malik's traplike mind.

"My lord," Ameen whispered near his ear,
"it's time to move away. Troops are coming."

Malik growled a response; he didn't want
to leave, but he knew he must. Those ground
troops would have dogs with them and dogs
would find them. Tucking his binoculars away,
he got to his feet.

"Where to, my lord?" Ameen asked.

"A change of plans," he told the teenage soldier. "We're going to Kabul…."

Thirty minutes after completing the flight
check list, Emma had taken the Apache off the
tarmac. The shaking and shuddering was famil-
iar and soothing to her. She'd felt the Taliban

nearby. She'd not seen them, but she instinctively knew they were close. Emma wondered if Khalid was testing her flight skills. After all, he'd been in Apaches for four years and she had only one year of combat beneath her belt.

At eight thousand feet under a sunny April-afternoon sky, Emma relaxed to a degree. Still, she was tense about going to Shaheen's home. This was out of normal military protocol. She had no experience with Afghans except in the villages, and Shaheen was much more powerful than those people who survived in the wild mountains along the border.

"Do you like dogs?" Khalid asked through the intercom.

Emma scowled. Now, what was this all about? Shaheen had the ability to rock her world. "Dogs?" What did dogs have to do with them? It was the last conversation she would think of having with this pilot. If nothing else, Khalid was turning out to be one surprise after another.

"Yes, dogs."

"Why are we talking about them?" Emma demanded, automatically looking around outside the cockpit.

"So you will be well-prepared when I open the door to my family's villa. My father raises some of the finest salukis in the world. Two years ago, he gifted me with Ayesha, a female with a black coat, white chest and cinnamon-colored legs and underbelly. My father gave her to me shortly after Najela was murdered. The dog helped me in ways I can't explain. She gave me back my life and brought me through the darkest tunnel with her love and devotion."

Not wanting to be swayed by his words, Emma swung her gaze across the instrument panel out of ingrained habit. The chances of attack were minimal, but she never completely let down her guard. "I'm sure I can handle your dog," she said, laughing. "Hey, it's kinda nice to have a dog around. We have a few base mongrels that we feed, but they're wild and you can't pet them. I'm always leaving scraps outside my tent for a black dog that comes by every night looking for something to eat. If I try to walk toward him, he takes off at a run and disappears. I've learned to put the food in a pie tin, close up my tent and not try to befriend him."

"Ah, you are a true lover of animals, too. That speaks highly of your heart, Captain Cantrell." Khalid's job in the front seat was to keep watch on the two video screens in front of him. There wasn't much chance of attack at this altitude, but you could never quite relax on the job. He was intensely curious about Emma, but hesitant. She was a by-the-book military officer. Giving her a rose had been a misstep. Khalid had hoped it would open a door to signify a good, working relationship, but Emma had taken it all wrong.

Worriedly, Khalid realized he'd set them on an awkward course with one another. And he desperately needed a woman pilot who could fulfill his vision to inspire the little Afghan girls. How to fix what had already gone wrong? She didn't sound very interested in his dog story, either.

Brows dipping, Khalid asked himself why he was so interested in Emma. She was a tough military combat pilot. Her record showed her abilities and fine skills. He got the feeling she really didn't like him at all and was just tolerating the situation. Maybe it was the attack this morning that had set her off. He shrugged his shoulders to ease them of tension. He simply didn't know how to deal with Captain Cantrell. Most people melted beneath his charm and sincere smile. But all it did to her was make her retreat, becoming stony and unreadable. As his U.S. military pilot friends would say, he'd blown it.

How to repair things between them? He'd spent years in the States being educated. He knew Americans. Khalid sighed. Emma made him feel like a joyous young man. That wouldn't work here. Khalid turned his attention to the screens and did an automatic scan, looking for possible SAM missiles. Taking a deep breath, he hoped what he was about to say wouldn't turn her away from him.

"I did a little research on you, Captain. Your family has a history of service," Khalid said.

Something had told her that as easy-going as Khalid appeared, he was a man who researched the details of any situation.

"Yes, the Trayherns have given military service to their country since they arrived here two hundred years earlier. My mother, Alyssa, was a Trayhern before she married Clay Cantrell, my father. It's a tradition for the Trayhern children, if they want, to go into the military of their choice and serve at least four to six years, depending upon whether they are officers or enlisted. We're very proud of our family's service and sacrifice," Emma said tensely.

"You should be. I'm very impressed, Captain.

That's very Sufi-like, to serve others. My Irish mother would say it is what you owe to life. That we all owe others. We can't live life alone or separate ourselves from the poor and suffering."

Emma moved uncomfortably around in her seat. Talking to Khalid was like a minefield. She didn't really want to know anything about him. All she wanted was to do a good job on this mission and then get back to base camp, her military record clean once more. Clearing her throat, she said, "She sounds like a wonderful, giving person much like my mother, Alyssa."

"My mother has red hair and brown eyes," Khalid informed her. "She's an obstetrician and she has set up clinics throughout Afghanistan with the help of her church's ongoing donations. She has spent from age twenty-eight to the present here in Afghanistan. The good she has done is tremendous. I think you must know many Afghan women die during childbirth. Most women have an average of seven children. And one out of eight women dies in childbirth. Very few villages have health care available to them."

"That's so sad," Emma said as she banked the Apache to start a descent into Bagram. They had left the mountains, and now the dry, yellow plains where Bagram air base sat spread out before them. "I can't believe how many women lose their lives. It's horrific. I heard from Major Klein, my C.O., that there are Sufi medical doctors who have devoted their lives to the villages along the border."

"Ah yes," Khalid said, brightening, "Doctors Reza and Sahar Khan. I've met them a number of times. My mother works with them through her mission. They are truly brave. Because they are Sufi and giving service and trying to help the border villages from the farthest south to the farthest north of our country, the Taliban constantly tries to kill them. The only way the Taliban keeps hold over our people is through

fear, retaliation and murder." His voice deepened. "Reza and Sahar have a strong calling.
As Sufis they render aid and help wherever they
can. Reza is a doctor of internal medicine and
surgery. His sister, Sahar, is an obstetrician. I
cannot tell you how many women's lives she has
saved. They drive a Land Rover that is beaten
up and very old. I have offered to buy them a
new one, but they said no."

"Why?"

"Because it would stand out like a sore thumb
and the Taliban could find them more easily.
In January of each year they start in the south
of Afghanistan and then they drive along the
border from village to village offering their
medical services for free. By the time June
comes, they have reached the northernmost part
of our country, and they turn around and drive
back down through the same villages. Each village gets visits twice a year, except of course,

the most northern one, but they stay two weeks there to ensure everyone in that village is properly cared for."

"Who funds them?"

"I do," Khalid said. "I also coordinate with several American charities who give them medical supplies. Money's only importance is how it is spent to help others."

Emma said nothing, easing the Apache down to three thousand feet. "That's gutsy, and talk about sacrifice, those two doctors should get medals of valor." Obviously, this officer was generous with his money. Brody's bragging came to mind. Was Khalid bragging to impress her? Something told her he was, and she became even more wary.

Snorting, Khalid said, "The central government refuses to acknowledge their sacrifice to our people. They aren't very happy about Sufis, either. They barely tolerate them."

"Why are Sufis so targeted?" Emma asked. She saw Bagram air base coming up. It was huge and lay on the flat, dirt plain with Kabul about ten miles away. The city glittered in the sunlight. Kabul wasn't that safe, either. The Taliban had infiltrated the city and it was dangerous for any American, military or civilian, to be there without an armed escort.

"What mystic group hasn't been a target?" he asked rhetorically. "Ah, Bagram is below us. We'll be on the ground in a few minutes."

She heard veiled excitement in his voice. Emma paid attention to the air controller giving her landing instructions. Tension accumulated in her shoulders. She really didn't want to go to Shaheen's home. It felt like a trap to her, but Khalid was her boss. If he wrote her up for a glowing commendation after this six-month gig, she'd have a revived military career in front of her. And Emma wanted nothing more than to expunge that black eye she'd given to the Trayhern family, once and for all.

"Come," Khalid said, gesturing toward a large parking lot inside Bagram air base. "My car is over there."

The roar of jets taking off shook the air until it vibrated around them. As Emma walked at Khalid's side, her bag in her left hand, dark aviator glasses in place, she felt nervous. At the Ops desk where they'd filled out the required landing flight forms, everyone seemed to know him. He had joked and laughed with many of the enlisted personnel behind the desk. His sincerity and concern for each of them was obvious. Emma saw how every man and woman glowed beneath his charisma. Brody Parker had done that, too. It seemed people who weren't as rich as he was were always enamored with him. Emma had realized later it had been because they knew he was rich.

As she walked down the line of cars, Emma reminded herself that Khalid was dangerous to her heart. He was far too likable a person. Frowning, she saw him take keys from his pocket and click them toward a Land Rover. The vehicle was a dark-green one that had plenty of dents and scrapes all over its body. In fact, there was a lot of dirt and mud on it, too.

"Hop in," Khalid invited, opening the rear so they could throw all their flight gear into the back.

Emma slid into the passenger side and put on the seat belt. The dashboard was dusty. She wondered if Khalid's home looked like his car.

Tension thrummed through Khalid as he drove through the security gates of Bagram after showing his identity card. "Have you been in the city of Kabul before?"

Emma watched him drive with care. "Yes, I have, but only with an Afghan escort on a day trip. When I fly in here, I remain on base for safety reasons." He looked around constantly. In fact, they both had their side arms on the seat between them. She knew attacks were frequent in Kabul. The road leading up to the base was asphalted, but soon they were on another highway with plenty of potholes to dodge. Heavy traffic came and went from the busy main air base that served the country.

"Not many Americans wander off Bagram," Khalid murmured, nodding. "And with good reason. They are targets. One day I hope that our country will be free of the Taliban and you can see the beauty of it."

Emma was as alert as he was, keeping a hand on her .45 pistol. Too many cars were attacked by the Taliban. That Khalid was a marked man only increased the chances that they could be attacked.

Khalid motioned with his long hand toward the city. "My parents' villa is on the outskirts, upon a small hill ringed with thick, almost impenetrable brush. I also employ guards at the base of the hill." He grimaced. "Unfortunately, anyone who is rich is an automatic target. But you will be safe at our compound. Ten-foot-high stucco walls completely surround our home. It's all one story so that it is hidden behind the walls. There is a metal gate at the entrance and a guard is always on duty. Each window has an ornamental grate across it to prevent break-ins. The front door is wrought iron, too."

"I don't know how anyone could live this way," Emma muttered. She saw Khalid give his characteristic shrug.

"We have generations of Afghans with PTSD, post traumatic stress disorder. We all have it," he said, glancing at Emma. "It's just a question of how bad it is and how much of your life it stains."

Shaking her head, she said, "I've always valued being born in the U.S., but after being over here and seeing the poverty, the murders and constant threats that your people live under, I feel very, very fortunate in comparison."

"Yes, I was grateful for my years I spent in your country," Khalid said. He swung off on a dirt road that led up to a small knoll in the distance. The road was rough and rutted because of the spring rains. "The seven years I spent there Americanized me a great deal." He flashed her a sudden grin. "I really miss American French fries."

For a moment, Emma's heart melted. His smile was dazzling and she felt the full effects of it. "You seem very Americanized. Your English is flawless and you use our slang, Captain Shaheen."

Khalid drove around some potholes, the ruts deep, dry and hard. The Land Rover crept forward. "I love America. I love what she stands for. I want my people to have a democracy just like yours. While I studied at Princeton, I truly understood what democracy was for the first time. I brought my passion back here and Kinah and I have worked ever since to bring our country closer to that vision we hold in our hearts."

"It's a vision worth holding," Emma agreed, hearing the fierce, underlying emotion in Khalid's voice. There was no question he loved this desert country. Emma studied the rounded hill coming up. The shrubs were thick and dark green from the base up to the top of greenish-brown stucco walls. The color of the walls blended into the earthen landscape. If she hadn't been looking for the walls, she probably would have missed them. She wondered what it was like for Khalid and his sister to grow up here under such constant threats. Her admiration for him grew.

The bearded guard at the front entrance opened the gate and saluted Khalid. The sentry stepped aside as Khalid returned the salute and drove the Land Rover into the three-car garage.

The automatic door started downward as he eased out of the vehicle.

Emma followed suit. They gathered their gear and he took her to a side door.

"Prepare yourself," he said, a glimmer in his eyes as he opened the door.

Emma didn't have time. The dog, a saluki, Ayesha, rushed out the door, barking joyously around them, her thick, long tail wagging with happiness. It was impossible for Emma to remain stiff and stoic. Khalid had been right: Ayesha would lick her fingers off her hand if allowed to do so.

Wiping her wet fingers on the side of her flight suit, Emma and Ayesha bounded over the white-tiled hall with its cool, pale-green walls. Khalid's laughter and playfulness around the saluki automatically made Emma's heart pound a little harder. Truly, Ayesha was a faithful companion to the Apache pilot who petted her fondly as she danced and pranced at his side.

The hall flowed in three different directions. Khalid pointed to the left. "Your suite is the second door on the left. My dear housekeeper, Rasa, has promised you will be comfortable while you visit us. If there's anything you need, just press the buzzer on the inside of the door, and she will come to assist you."

"And you, Captain?" Emma asked.

"I'm going to my suite, get out of my uniform, grab a shower and I'll meet you in our courtyard in an hour. There's much to show you before we have dinner at 8:00 p.m. tonight."

Dinner. Her spirit sank. Emma didn't want to spend too much time with this pilot. He was too mesmerizing. Ayesha bounced around Khalid, her tongue lolling out of her long muzzle, her dark-brown eyes alight with worship for her master. "I'll see you later," she said, more tersely than she meant it to be. Emma wished mightily for a bathtub, but they weren't to be found anywhere. At base camp, there were only showers. Her flight boots thunked with a slight echo down the highly polished white-, brown- and orange-tiled hall.

The door to her suite was ajar. Emma pushed it open and walked in. What she saw made her gasp with delight. The suite looked like a five-star hotel room! Across the king-sized bed was a gorgeous lavender-and-white star quilt. And on the wall above it hung an art fabric collage of a Rocky Mountain meadow filled with colorful wildflowers. Setting her bags on the bed, Emma looked around, dazed by the quality of the furniture, the decorations and the sense of peace that filled the room.

Her mahogany dresser was an antique. She ran her hand across the polished surface and figured it had to be from either North America or perhaps Europe. As Emma opened one of the drawers, she noticed the dovetailing on each side, another sign of quality craftsmanship. She tucked away her few clothes, keeping out her silky pink pajamas and her own washcloth. Emma had learned a long time ago to carry one with her since many countries didn't provide them.

The pale-lavender walls matched the beautiful quilt on her bed. Fresh flowers in a brass vase adorned the mahogany coffee table that stood between a small purple sofa and a wing chair. Soft music played from a radio. Doilies and a long embroidered runner lay across the top of the dresser. The furnishings gave the room a 1930s flavor. She felt as if she'd walked back in time to an era when everything was made by hand. Even the rugs on either side of the bed seemed to have been handmade from scraps of cloth that had been wound into ropes and then anchored together.

Walking through another open door, Emma sighed. With a Jacuzzi bathtub, the bathroom was as large as her bedroom! She gazed at it longingly. Mentally, she blessed Khalid's westernized parents for their thoughtfulness toward their visitors. There was also a large glass-and-tile shower. The blue tiles on the walls were hand-painted with colorful wildflowers. Emma recognized some of them, others she did not. She walked closer to study them. Some were from the U.S., for sure. Others were jungle flowers and orchids.

A washcloth and a bright-yellow fuzzy towel had been folded on a nearby table. Lavender-colored soap sat in a white ceramic dish. She picked up a bar and inhaled the fragrance. It was jasmine, one of her favorite scents. Did Khalid know that? How could he? Emma replaced the soap and turned, suddenly feeling horribly trapped by the assignment. First things first. Emma noticed a range of hair products near the white porcelain sink. She would draw a luxurious bath, soak and then wash her hair in the shower. Still in mild shock over the plush suite, she once again reminded herself that Khalid was a man full of surprises.

What next? Emma wasn't sure. She quickly
shed her boots and uniform and turned on the
faucet to fill the Jacuzzi tub. As she sat on the
edge of the tub and swirled her fingers through
the warm water, she felt her heart shrink with
fear and dread. What if Khalid made a move on
her? Emma could swear he liked her, but so far,
he hadn't done anything off limits. The rose told
her he was flirting. Did he see her as nothing
more than a woman to chase and try to catch in
the next six months? Brody had done something
similar; he'd chased her for four months before
she'd agreed to a date.

Careful. You can't get involved with him. You
have your family to think of first. You have to
redeem the Trayhern's good name. Never mind
Khalid is warm, personable, humorous and
kind. Or rich. Groaning, Emma closed her eyes
for a moment. This mission was much worse
than she'd ever realized.

Chapter 4

"Come," Khalid invited Emma as she walked into the spacious kitchen, "let's go to the garage. I have my storehouse in there." He tried to ignore the fact that she was now in civilian clothes, her red hair still damp from the shower and falling like fiery lava around her proud shoulders. Instead of a baggy olive-green flight suit, Emma now wore a tangerine-colored T-shirt with dark-brown trousers. On her, they looked good. Too good.

"I'll follow," Emma said firmly, gesturing

for him to take the lead. Emma could smell the wonderful odor of lamb cooking with spices in the oven. With how Khalid's light-blue polo shirt showed the breadth of his chest, Emma kept distance between them. He was just too much of a temptation.

Khalid opened the door to the storehouse and stepped aside to allow Emma to enter. He turned on the lights. Emma halted and stared around the cavernous three-car garage that held only the Land Rover right now. Along the walls in neat rows were thousands of books and boxes of educational items such as crayons, pencils, pens and notebooks.

"This is our vision," Khalid said, closing the door and walking into the room. "Kinah and I bought state-of-the-art printing machines. We gathered a group of Afghan widows and trained them to print out the books for the children." He went to one aisle, pulled out a book and opened it. "We've not only employed six women who had no way to earn any money. Now they are our printers and publisher. The books are written by the best authorities in education, according to Kinah. She worked a year to produce Pashto-written texts and pictures from grades one through twelve. It was a momentous challenge."

Emma nodded but remained distant. She made sure there was plenty of space between them. She heard the pride in Khalid's voice for his innovating and hard-working sister. "This is a major undertaking."

Khalid nodded and slid the book back onto the shelf. "Yes, it is." He gazed down at Emma and had a maddening urge to tangle his fingers in her damp red hair, which curled softly around her face. Did she know how fetching she looked with that coverlet of copper freckles across her nose and cheeks? Emma wore no make up, but didn't need any. She was beautiful just as she was, Khalid's heart whispered to him. But since he was marked for death, there was no way to fall in love with any woman, not even someone as tempting as Emma Cantrell. He focused on showing Emma the large room of supplies. "Once we begin Operation Book Worm, all the supplies will come from this location. They will be marked, packed by another group of widows and then sent by truck to Bagram for us. From there, we put them aboard our CH-47 and fly them out to the villages."

"And your sister Kinah?" Emma asked. "Where is she in all of this?"

"Right now my sister is working with leaders of the first ten villages along the border where we will set up the schools. She's taking a roster of each child, his or her age, and how many children will be in each school." Khalid said fondly, "My sister is a tempest. She never sits still. Kinah's a fierce warrior for peace and the education of our people. She's a fighter who has vision, strength, intelligence and courage."

"She'd have to have all those things to do what she's doing," Emma agreed grimly, looking around in awe at the room. "Her life is always on the line out there. I'm sure you know that."

Darkness came to Khalid's normally sparkling blue eyes.

"Too aware. I have hired two of the best security guards I can find, but I still worry about her. She refuses to wear a flak jacket, which concerns me. We have ancient enemies out there." His voice lowered. "I know Malik is hunting us, Emma. He's just waiting to spring a trap to capture either or both of us. I worry it will happen when Kinah is alone and unable to defend herself...."

"And yet, you have said Asad Malik has promised your death." Emma looked around. "Where are *your* bodyguards?"

Khalid shrugged. "Now, you sound like my sister, Captain. She is always on me to have them."

"Thanks for the tour, Khalid." Emma sounded less military and slightly breathless. That irritated her a whole lot. Emma felt an unexpected yearning for him that was like a flowing stream that turned into a wild river within her. Khalid was too good to be true. Brody had never been a humanitarian and that's where they were different. In Emma's eyes and heart, Khalid was a true hero, fighting to lift his people out of abject poverty. He had the money, the position and resources to make it happen. There was a generosity so deep within him that it made Emma stand in awe of Khalid. How many men had she met that had all these qualities? Not many. All the more reason to remain at arm's length from this fierce Afghan warrior.

"You're welcome, Captain Cantrell. Now," he said, glancing down at his watch, "I believe Rasa will have our dinner ready for us."

Emma walked toward the door, dreading the meal. Hopefully, she asked, "Are you going to split us up? I'll eat in the women's quarter and you in the men's?" In the Muslim world, men and women ate separately.

Khalid laughed and walked quickly to open the door before she got to it. "No. You are American and I honor the fact that Americans sit as families together. We'll eat in the dining room." He saw a wariness in her eyes and added, "Does this meet with your approval?" No longer could he afford to assume anything about this woman.

Emma kept her sedate demeanor. "This is not military protocol, Captain Shaheen. To tell you the truth, I'm a little uncomfortable with it all." There, the truth was out. Emma noticed the genuine concern in his face and how much her words had hurt him. She knew how important it was for an Afghan to be a host. "But I'll deal with it."

"Yes?" Khalid said hopefully. "For I have no wish to offend you again."

"I'm not offended." Emma hoped she'd smoothed the situation over enough so they could have a quick dinner and she could make a run for her suite.

Asad Malik arrived in Kabul at 9:00 p.m. He and his men had met with a local Taliban sheik at a village outside Camp Bravo. He'd loaned them two pickup trucks so that they could speed their way to Kabul. The stars were bright and beautiful above him as they pulled up at the bottom of the hill where the Shaheen family home sat.

They got out of their pickups and quietly assembled near Malik. He put on a special pair of night goggles stolen from an American soldier during a heated battle. He liked these goggles because, suddenly, night became day. Everything was green and grainy, but he could see. This was the first time he'd ever been this close to the Shaheen estate. As he used binoculars and began a survey of the home, he realized it was going to be very hard to attack.

Ameen, his second in command, came up to him. "My lord, is there a way we can assault the home?"

Malik growled under his breath, "There's heavy brush all around the hill. At the top, there is a ten-foot wall. And on top of the wall is concertina barbed wire." Dropping the binoculars, he handed them to the young man, who wore a worn brown turban on his head. "Stay here. I'm going to look around. With these goggles, I'll be able to see much more." He picked up his rifle and melted into the night, leaving his men standing quietly by the trucks.

Emma walked down the hallway and back into the kitchen. A short, black-haired woman in a long dark blue gown stood at the oven. She wore oven mitts as she pulled out the lamb and placed it on the counter. When Emma saw the housekeeper's face she bit down on her lower lip. The whole left side was terribly twisted and scarred, as if severely burned. What had happened to her? Emma had no time to think about this because Khalid cupped his hand beneath her right elbow and guided her into a huge dining room with its crystal chandelier hanging over a long, rectangular mahogany table.

Once out of earshot, Emma whispered, "Captain Shaheen, what happened to Rasa? Her face is horribly scarred."

Khalid pulled out the chair at the end of the table for her. He dropped his voice. "Rasa lived in a border village. She was fighting to get a school started for girls. Rasa was well-educated and a fighter for women's rights."

Emma sat down and looked up to see darkness in Khalid's eyes. He took a chair on her right and sat down. "Malik, our enemy, heard of Rasa's efforts and he brought his thugs into the village. They found her and poured acid all over her face and told her to stop thinking about educating girls. She was told that women were more stupid than the donkeys that hauled the loads of firewood into the village."

Emma was horrified. "My God, I'm so sorry for Rasa."

He picked up her gold linen napkin and handed it to her. "Rasa lost the sight in her left eye, too. When my father, who was trying to bring education to the villages so long ago, found Rasa, he brought her here, to Kabul. He paid for all of her medical needs. At that time, Rasa was only eighteen years old. She was so grateful that she begged my father to allow her to be the permanent housekeeper for our family. She wanted to repay my father for all his generosity toward her. Rasa remains blind in that eye to this day, and there is nothing that could be done for her. But her face is much improved over what it was at first."

"This isn't right, Khalid. Malik is evil."

Opening his napkin, Khalid nodded. "He's a murderer. One day, I will meet him on the plain of combat."

Startled by his words, Emma realized she was seeing the warrior side of Khalid for the first time. He was a combatant now, his eyes narrowed and dark, his full, expressive mouth thinned with tension. Emma felt the chill of his rage. The light-hearted Khalid had disappeared. Now she understood a little more why this man had been chosen by the U.S. Army for Apache combat helicopter training. This aviator was a consummate hunter, like the legendary and mystical snow leopards who lived in the Kush mountains.

Taking a shaky breath, Emma asked under her breath, "Does Rasa know English?"

"No." Khalid gave her a pleading look. "When Rasa comes to serve us, please do not look into her eyes. She never meets your gaze. Her eyes are always downcast and she speaks so softly that at times, I have a hard time hearing her."

Heart aching for Rasa, Emma felt how the woman's spirit had been broken by Malik's attack upon her. "Of course," she promised. "I don't wish to make her uncomfortable, Captain."

Khalid nodded and looked toward the arched entrance that led to the kitchen. "Rasa is painfully aware that no man would ever take her as his bride. She hides beneath a burka so that no one can see her damaged face when she shops in Kabul for us. I have tried over the years to convince her she is not ugly, that she has a beautiful heart and soul. And that any man would overlook her physical face for the unscarred beauty of her heart," he sighed, "but she will not believe me. I have brought potential suitors here for her, but she shuns them." Shrugging, Khalid said, "I've given up at this point."

"Is Rasa happy here?" Emma asked, touched

by Khalid's obvious grief over Rasa's suffering. He seemed to hold back unknown emotions.

"Very happy. She has adopted us as her family." Khalid saw Rasa coming from the kitchen with a tray of steaming food. "We'll speak later," he said in a quiet tone.

"Of course," Emma said.

Malik crept silently along the road leading to the estate. Crouching, his AK-47 in his right hand, the butt resting on the earth, he eyed two turbaned guards at a ten-foot wrought-iron black gate. They weren't like most security guards. No, these two bearded men were alert and looking around. Malik knew he was well-hidden by the brush on the dirt road.

After waiting five more minutes, Malik crept into the brush. It was thick but negotiable. He was tall and wiry and able to step softly and not raise alarm. Sitting down, he observed the gate head-on. The guards never left it. He could hear them talking in the distance. They carried AK-47s with two bandoliers of ammo crisscrossing their powerful chests. Judging from how they carried themselves, these were Afghan warriors and not the drivel from Kabul who couldn't fight a fly.

Slowly turning his head, Malik decided to continue to move slowly and quietly around the hill to see if there was another entrance to the estate.

"And so," Khalid said, pointing to the papers spread out on the table after dinner, "this is the full concept of our efforts."

It was nearly 10:00 p.m. as Emma pored over all the information about Operation Book Worm. "This is impressive." She glanced at Khalid, who sat to her right. "How long did it take you two to figure this out?"

"Four years," Khalid murmured. Emma's hair was dry now and curled in crimson around her freckled face. Did she know how beautiful and utterly natural a woman she was? Khalid itched to understand her on a more personal level. He knew she was single because he had looked at her personnel jacket. She had been suggested as the right person to partner with him on this effort. And she was.

It was on the tip of Khalid's tongue to ask if she had a significant other. Just because Emma was single didn't mean she was available. And why was he even thinking in that direction? He could be killed at any moment by Asad Malik. Unconsciously, Khalid touched his chest where his heart resided. Was he finished grieving for his fiancée? Was he returning to life as a man with yearnings and needs? Was his wounded heart truly healed and now calling for him to find another woman who could fulfill his dreams? But that could never happen. Khalid would never put another woman in the sites of Malik.

Emma saw the odd look in Khalid's eyes. What was he thinking? She nervously gathered up the papers and handed them over to him. "It's late," she said firmly. "I know we're getting up early tomorrow. Kinah will be here at 0800? Right?"

"Yes, my sister is flying in tomorrow morning. She'll have the information we require. Then, the widows will be driven over here and, based upon Kinah's assessments, we'll get busy filling orders for each village and boxing them up. Then, you and I will trailer them to the CH-47 assigned to us at Bagram Air Force Base."

Emma rose. "Sounds good, Captain. I'll see you tomorrow morning." All evening she had felt as if Khalid wanted a warm, intimate conversation with her. Oh, nothing overt. Subtle, just as Brody had been. Emma rose from the table and smoothed her slacks.

Khalid quickly stood with her. There was confusion in Emma's green gaze. Why? There was a wariness in her expression as if he had somehow, once more, breached officer-to-officer protocol. Should he apologize? Khalid had treated her with courtesy and kept all conversations about the mission, nothing personal, during dinner. He didn't want to chase Emma off this operation by unmilitary behavior toward her.

Malik hissed beneath his breath. There was no entrance other than the one gate to Shaheen's estate. Making his way back to his men who were patiently crouched and holding their weapons, he took off the goggles. Ameen approached, a hopeful look on his darkened face.

"I will not throw away our lives on trying to get into that castle," he told his men. "I swear blood vengeance on Khalid Shaheen, but this will not be the place to settle that score." Lifting his hand, he gestured sharply to the trucks. "Mount up. We're going back to the base camp.

We will watch Shaheen's movements from there and figure out what he's up to now."

By the time Emma got up and dressed in a fresh flight uniform, Kinah and Khalid were already in the dining room having breakfast. Emma had slept hard. She realized how safe she felt in this villa compared to the base camp where mortars would sometimes be lobbed at them by the Taliban. Rubbing her eyes, she smiled a welcome as Kinah rose to greet her.

"Ah, you are the red-haired pilot Khalid spoke of," Kinah said, getting up, her hand extended to meet Emma. "I'm Kinah Shaheen. Khalid's little sister." She grinned mischievously and glanced back at her brother who sat at the table.

Emma grasped Kinah's long, graceful hand. She had nearly waist-length black hair shot through with red strands, green eyes that Emma was sure came from her Irish mother and full lips. Kinah was dressed in a traditional black Muslim gown.

"Hi, Kinah. I'm Captain Emma Cantrell. Nice to meet you."

Kinah stepped back and placed her hands on her hips. "Khalid, shame on you! You did not tell me how lovely this American woman pilot is!" She gave Emma a wink.

Emma decided Kinah was every bit the trickster that Khalid was. It must be that wicked Irish sense of humor in their DNA.

Dressed in his flight suit, Khalid made sounds of protest. "Beloved sister, Captain Cantrell is here as an envoy from the States. Why would I speak of her obvious beauty?" For once, he wished outgoing Kinah would not embarrass Emma. She might bolt and refuse to work on the mission.

As she walked to the table, Emma noticed that a third breakfast setting was there for her. They had not yet eaten and apparently were waiting for her to arrive; such were their manners. "I don't know about you, but I'd love some chai. I need to wake up," she told them, sitting down. Kinah sat at the head of the table this time, her brother on her right and Emma on the left.

"Indeed," Kinah said with a smile, "I believe Rasa is fixing three cups of chai as we speak." She reached over and gripped Emma's lower arm. "We are truly grateful for your presence, Captain Cantrell."

"Call me Emma." There was such warmth in the woman that Emma found herself climbing out of her military decorum.

"Wonderful," Kinah said. "I don't like standing on protocol, either. Please call me Kinah. When we're out in the field together, you must consider yourself a part of our family." She gestured to herself and her brother.

"Well…" Khalid choked, giving his vivacious sister a pained look. "We're in the military,

Kinah. I can't just call her by her first name out there."

"Pooh!" Kinah waggled her finger into Khalid's face. "We must appear bonded and friends, brother. After all, it was my idea to bring in an American woman pilot."

Emma saw Rasa come, head down, eyes trained on the floor, bearing a tray with three steaming cups of chai. She could smell the cinnamon and nutmeg fragrance wafting upward in the steam. Kinah's words caught her attention.

"Oh?"

Kinah took her chai and warmly thanked Rasa, who murmured back in Pashto. "I believe," Kinah said, resting her elbows on the table, the chai in her hands, "that little girls out in these villages need to see two strong women from two different cultures." Her eyes sparkled and she said in a whisper, "How else are my little girls to know they can dream as big as their hearts? They see me as an educator. They see you as a woman in the military who can fly a helicopter, who is an officer and who is fully capable. You see," she said, sipping her chai delicately, "little girls in the villages are often told they can't dream of being anything. They see you and me, Emma. They will get it very quickly that they *can* dream! They *can* set a goal through learning to read and write."

Moved by Kinah's passion, Emma said, "I hadn't thought of it in that way, but you're right. Leading by example."

Nodding, Kinah said, "Exactly. I expect you to give a little talk at some point, after we have the schools set up. I would like you to share how you became a pilot. What made you yearn to fly? What dreams did you have as a little girl that fueled your desire to fly a helicopter? You see," Kinah said, smiling softly, "little girls have wings of imagination. You can instill them to imagine whatever it is they desire to become."

Emma smiled a little and sipped her chai. Clearly, Kinah was a force of nature. Compared to Khalid, she was a ball of energy, hardly able to sit still, her hands always gesturing and her eyes fierce with passion. Khalid paled in comparison to his dynamo sister. The fact that Khalid was the rudder to Kinah's ship of dreams made Emma respect him even more. She could see the doting, loving look on Khalid's face for his beloved sister. She wondered if Khalid took after his Sufi father and Kinah her Irish mother. Clearly, the fire belonged to Kinah.

Emma could understand why Khalid adored his sister. Kinah, although in traditional Afghan dress, was far more a feminist that Emma ever had been. "I wonder if you picked up on your Irish mother's DNA? You're a missionary of a different sort," Emma said. "Is it not a religious calling as much as a humanitarian effort that drives you?"

"Precisely," Kinah said, nodding her head, her

dark curls moving across her back. "I may only be small but I am a giant who stands over most others because my heart is connected to my dreams." She gave Khalid a warm, loving look. "And my Sufi brother knows well that when our hearts are aligned with our passions, we can accomplish miracles."

Once Rasa completed delivering their breakfast, Kinah called her over, stood up and gave the housekeeper a warm hug and thanked her. Rasa was bright-red, obviously uneasy and quickly scuttled back to the safety of her kitchen.

Kinah sat down. "You see, women like Rasa deserve more from life than having acid thrown in their face by those bastards."

Emma nearly choked on her eggs. Kinah's language startled her.

Khalid groaned again and gave Emma look of apology for his sister's bad language.

Kinah merely laughed and ate heartily.

Emma bowed her head and ate her food. She felt caught up in a whirlwind in Kinah's presence. But it was a good one. Now, she grasped Khalid's worry for his fierce, passionate sister. And given that Asad Malik hated this family, Emma understood why. If Malik ever encountered Kinah, it would be a battle of life and death. Kinah was no wilting lily. She would fight to the death rather than allow Malik to rape her, cut her throat or throw acid in her face. No, Malik would have met his equal and Emma bet that Kinah would win the day, if not the war itself.

Chapter 5

Emma tried to still her excitement and fear as she piloted the CH-47 toward their first village. The vibration rippling through the bird soothed her. The April morning was crisp and clear. They had left Bagram with boxes of educational supplies. In the rear, on the nylon seats along the fuselage, sat Kinah. The load master, Tech. Sgt. Brad Stapleton, all of twenty-two years old, also sat in the back. He would be responsible for unloading their supplies once they arrived at the border village. To her left was Khalid, her copilot on this mission. They had just flown past her black ops base camp, and were now heading toward Asmar and then on to their final destination, Do Bandi.

Asmar was a larger village on a dirt road and further away from the border with Pakistan. Do Bandi was closer to the border and had been protected by A-teams, army Special Forces comprised of ten men. These teams lived in the village, rotating out every thirty days when a new team came in to replace it. Khalid and Kinah felt this village was safer than most and a good one to cut their teeth on. Emma couldn't disagree. There were a lot of logistics and this was their first trial-and-error run.

"Do the village elders know we're flying in this morning?" Emma asked Khalid over the intercom.

"Yes. The A-team stationed there received permission from the chieftain two weeks ago for us to visit him." He flipped her a thumbs-up with his gloved hand. "It's a go." He grinned.

Khalid reminded her of an excited little boy. Emma wasn't sure who was more anticipatory: him or his restless, dynamic sister, Kinah. Neither had barely slept last night, they were so "charged up and ready to rock 'n' roll," as Khalid had put it this morning over breakfast. Emma had slept deeply and had had torrid dreams about Khalid. As a result, she'd awakened this morning in a sour mood. How to keep her boss at bay, do her job and not get involved were *her* logistical problems to solve.

Emma took the CH-47 down to one hundred feet as they approached the first range of snow-covered mountains. They would fly nap-of-the-earth, skimming at that low altitude up, down and around through mountain peaks and passes in order not to be fired upon by the Taliban. Any helicopter that didn't do this type of herky-jerky flying was a sure target for a Taliban rocket. Emma loved flying by the seat of her pants in the hulking, slow transport. The helo was sluggish, but it was steady beneath her hands, which gripped the cyclic and collective. Her intense focus was on skimming the earth and not getting nailed with a rock outcropping or brushing too close to a granite wall with the tips of the helo's rotors.

By the time they reached Do Bandi, which sat down at the north end of a narrow, green valley, the armpits on Emma's flight suit were wet with sweat. Her heart pounded, adrenaline coursing through her bloodstream. Every time she had to fly nap-of-the-earth, the percentage of a crash rose exponentially. It was life-and-death flying, as she and her cohorts called it. But there was no other choice, was there?

As Emma brought the transport in for a landing outside the village, the twin rotors kicked up thick, choking dust that billowed hundreds of feet into the air. A huddled group of elders hid behind the mud huts to protect themselves from flying dust and debris. The CH-47 hunkered down and Khalid quickly shut down the engines. Emma saw the A-team coming out of the shadows of the line of huts. They were the first to approach. Emma ordered the load master over the intercom to open up the helo.

"I'm bringing down the ramp," Stapleton told her. "A-team is approaching on the starboard side."

"Roger," Emma murmured. She heard the grating roar echo through the helo as the ramp began to descend. The helo vibrated and groaned.

Khalid unstrapped. He wore a Kevlar vest and a .45 pistol holstered across his chest. Grinning, he felt higher than a kite flying off a hill in Kabul. Kite-running was something he'd done as a child. He'd never won, but the exhilaration of flying a kite and then chasing it was always thrilling. That was how he felt now: anticipation and joy.

Pulling off her helmet after unstrapping, Emma quickly ran her fingers through her flattened hair. She'd tied her shoulder-length hair into a knot at the nape of her neck. From her right thigh pocket she pulled out a dark-green silk scarf known as a hijab, to wrap around her head. The hijab was a sign of respect to the Muslim Afghan people. Women did not go out into public without their heads being covered. She didn't mind fitting in, although Emma found it ironic in another way. Here she was, a modern-day combat helicopter pilot wearing a .45 strapped across her chest and a delicate, feminine scarf. It was April and cold so the scarf would keep her head warm.

"Ready?" Khalid asked, switching everything off in the cabin. His job as copilot was to power down the helo after it landed. His hands flew across the console, flipping switches and turning off the radios.

Emma turned in her seat. The groaning ramp came to a rest in the dirt with a "clunk."

"Ready," she said. She gave Kinah a thumbs-up, which meant it was all right to unstrap. The woman smiled and nodded, quickly removing the harness and getting to her feet. There were about fifty boxes in the hold of the transport. Only about half were actual school supplies. The rest were donations from America of clothing and shoes for the children. There were also medical items for the A-team sergeant who was responsible for the health of the villagers. Penicillin and other antibiotics were treasures out on the frontier and Emma knew their worth was as gold to the Afghan leaders. Antibiotics were desperately needed by all border villages, but few ever received them. Death by infection was a common way to die, unfortunately.

Kinah walked down the ramp. She was

dressed in a black wool robe with a bright red hijab over her thick, dark hair. She shook the hand of the captain of the A-team and then walked quickly toward the wall of old men, the elders of the village.

Emma could see her breath and knew that at this altitude, the temperature was still at freezing. She would be glad to see May arrive and warmth grudgingly coming back to these mountain villages. She had pulled on her thick, warm green nylon jacket and left it unzipped in order to reach for her .45 in case she needed it. Although Khalid felt this was a highly secure village, no one took it on faith. The Taliban had made repeated attacks on it, only to be repulsed by the A-team stationed here. The BJS Apache combat helicopters spewed out their bullets and rockets at the enemy when called in by the A-team to chase them away.

Khalid came to her side as she stood just

below the lip of the ramp. "Come, let me introduce you."

"Kinah already has the elders smiling," Emma observed, giving him a slight grin. "Your sister should run the United Nations."

Khalid laughed heartily. "My sister is a one-woman army, no question. She's like a laser-fired rocket—she knows her destination and nothing will stop her from reaching it." Khalid walked toward the huddled group near the huts. "I love my sister dearly. I worry about her, though. She disdains having guards to protect her."

Emma nodded. Today, Kinah had ordered her two Afghan guards to remain in Kabul. She did not want them near her on this first, important step of their education mission. And worse, Kinah would remain behind in the village after all the supplies were removed by the load master and the A-team members. She saw the worry banked in Khalid's eyes. Border villages were not safe and they never would be until the Afghanistan government turned its eyes and heart to them. These villages took the brunt of the Taliban attacks.

Emma stood at Khalid's side as he greeted the village elders in Pashto. She was glad she could understand what was being exchanged. There was much hand-shaking and touching of cheeks between Kinah, Khalid and the elders. Khalid ensured that Emma was introduced and she went through the same greetings with the elders. She could see that hope burned bright in their aged eyes. Not only was this village receiving protection from the A-team and the army from the air, but medicine was now available. The next step was education for their children. Emma knew that Afghans fiercely loved their children and wanted only the best for them.

Khalid turned to Emma. "Would you like to

work with the wives of the leaders to distribute the clothes and shoes?"

"Of course," Emma said. Behind the elders was a group of their wives dressed in burkas, only eye slits to see through. The burkas were only worn outside; in their homes, they came off. Emma went and introduced herself. She led the four women to the supplies being stacked outside the CH-47. There were fifteen boxes of clothes and shoes. She watched as the women reverently touched the cardboard boxes. Their voices were low and filled with excitement.

Khalid was busy for the next hour. It was important to get the helo unloaded and back into the air. They couldn't remain on the ground for fear of a Taliban attack. He'd lost sight of Emma, who had gone into the village with the women. The elders had chosen an empty mud hut for the school, which was where Kinah had gone with the boxes and many curious, excited children.

Finishing up, Khalid walked down the rutted main street with huts on either side. A donkey pulled a creaking cart, the owner walking beside the gray beast. He was heading down the slope below the village in search of firewood. Dogs barked and ran excitedly up and down the street.

Khalid remained anxious since the Taliban were always nearby; it was just a question of when they would sneak in to try and attack these good people. Leaping over several ruts, Khalid walked to the house of the chieftain, sure that Emma would be there. The children were all lined up at the door, giggling and expectant. Some of the children had shoes, others didn't. Mothers with their wriggling, restive children stood patiently, hidden beneath their burkas, waiting for their turns to get their children fitted for shoes.

Khalid squeezed through the door, and Emma realized how handsome he looked. His short black hair was mussed, giving him a boyish look. She forced herself to remain neutral toward him by repeating Brody's name in her head.

"Ready?" Khalid called to her over the noise of the children. The wives of the leaders had opened many of the shoe boxes. A child sat in a chair as the mother tried on pair after pair until they found the size to fit her child's feet.

"Yes," Emma called over the din. She turned and warmly thanked one of the wives and told her she had to go. The woman smiled and pressed her burka-covered cheek against Emma's. One thing Emma had learned was that if one could befriend Afghan people, they were loyal to the death. A fierce love welled up in her chest. These villagers had courage to survive despite the terror of the Taliban always skulking nearby, hidden and deadly.

"How about a quick lunch at your base

camp?" Khalid suggested on the way back to the unloaded helo.

She shrugged. There were so many fine lines to walk with him. Emma knew if she turned him down, he might get upset. For a C.O., an invitation was often an order. "Sure," she said.

"It's not a death sentence," Khalid teased her as they walked shoulder-to-shoulder down the main street. There was such struggle in Emma's face, and he tried to put her at ease.

"Captain, you have a dry sense of humor," Emma said.

He sighed and pressed his hand over his heart. "I've been so charged," he admitted, wishing for some relaxation between them.

Though she felt bad, Emma forced herself not to feel sorry for him. Khalid was her boss, pure and simple. She wanted high marks from him after this six-month gig. He obviously saw her reluctance.

Khalid performed the mandatory walk around

the helo, part of his copilot duties. He would look for anything loose, oil leaking or flight surfaces that weren't secure. Emma went directly to the cockpit. Sitting down in the right-hand seat, she got ready to perform the takeoff check list once Khalid finished his inspection tour outside the CH-47.

For the next five minutes, they were too busy to talk. Khalid called the black ops base and let them know they were taking off. Sometimes, an Apache helo would escort them, but today, there was high demand up north near Zor Barawul. The Taliban had launched another offensive against the village and it was currently being repulsed by a lot of air power. Their next stop tomorrow was that very village. Danger was always near.

"So," Khalid said as he sat opposite Emma in the chow hall back at base camp, "what would you tell the little girls about yourself?" He was obviously casting around for a way to ease the tension between them.

Emma had lifted her fork halfway to her mouth and stopped. She had spaghetti with meatballs. Khalid had the same, adding four pieces of buttered garlic bread, as well. She frowned momentarily, ate her food and considered his request. His question seemed innocent enough.

"I'd tell them that my family is a military one," she said between bites. "Nearly all the Trayhern children serve at least one tour in the service of their choice."

"So," Khalid said, relishing the warm garlic bread, "little girls would think that this career choice is expected?"

Emma shrugged. "I guess it is. My youngest sister, Casey, wasn't interested in being in the military. She joined the Forest Service and is a ranger currently stationed at Grand Tetons National Park in Wyoming."

"Is she considered an outcast?" Khalid wondered. While he hungered for a more personal connection, Khalid resisted his impulses.

Emma shook her head. "No, of course not. My Uncle Morgan Trayhern is fine with whatever we kids want to do with our lives. He loves Casey as much as any of the rest of us. His adopted daughter, Kamaria, never went into the military. She's a professional photographer and was a stringer for a number of top-flight news organizations around the world before she settled down at a Wyoming ranch."

"The girls would probably like to know how many children are in your family."

Emma smiled and explained. "Let's see. I'm the oldest. Then came the first set of twins, Athena and Juno. Two years after that, Casey and Selene. There are five daughters in our family. My mother loves the Greek myths so she named each one of us after a goddess. In my case, my middle name is Metis. She was a goddess and mother to Athena. Casey hated her name, Castalia, and so she shortened it to what it is now." Emma grinned. "My poor dad had five girls running under his feet, but my mom thought it was great," she laughed. "We're a very close, tight-knit family."

Khalid had watched her relax slightly and dared to ask a personal question. "Are you the only daughter with red hair?"

"No. My mother, Alyssa, said she has red hair and twins in her DNA. Two of my twin sisters, Casey and Selene, have red hair, too. Athena and Juno have my dad's black hair. Why?"

Khalid shared a slight smile with her. "I like the combination of your red hair and freckles. It makes you look like a young girl despite your being a mature woman, Captain."

Grimacing, Emma growled, "Don't remind me!" She sopped up some of the marinara sauce with her garlic bread. "All my life I've had to fight that little-girl look. I'll probably have to have gray hairs before anyone gets that I'm not a teenager."

Chuckling, Khalid felt his heart expand. He saw the righteous indignation gleaming in Emma's green eyes. Her mouth was beautifully shaped. He entertained the dream of someday kissing her, just to discover how soft and luscious she was. What was it about Emma that made him realize he was a man with needs once more?

As he twisted his spaghetti around his fork, Khalid asked, "They will probably ask if you have a man who loves you." He knew he was taking a chance with such a question. Emma's eyes flared with surprise. Khalid added a coaxing smile with his request, and her fine, thin red brows eased. He was glad he could influence her mood. Did he dare interpret that look to mean she was interested in him? Khalid felt torn. Half of him wanted a personal relationship with Emma. The other half did not want to put her life at risk.

Pushing her plate away, Emma picked up her mug of coffee. "No, not presently," she slowly admitted. And then the words leaped out of her mouth before she could stop them. "What about you?"

"I'm like you," Khalid offered.

"Because of Najela?" Emma guessed. She saw pain come to his eyes for a moment.

"Yes. I am just now realizing that I am ready to face life on the personal front again." Khalid did not say, *Because of you, I am inspired not only to live again, but to allow my heart to dream of you....*

Emma didn't know what to say. Clearly, Khalid liked her. She saw it in his hooded gaze, the desire banked in their blue depths. Paying strict attention to her coffee, she hoped the moment would pass.

"Now that we've started this mission," Khalid

said, "you are welcome to stay as my guest at our home in Kabul. You don't need to remain here at the base camp."

"No," Emma said with finality, "I want to stay here." *That way, you won't be so available.* She was afraid of herself. Afraid of what she might do because Khalid clearly desired her. The man was more than capable of sweet-talking her into something that couldn't—shouldn't—happen. Seeing the regret in his expression, Emma steeled herself against Khalid. The man oozed charm and sensuality.

"Well," Khalid said, setting his emptied plate to one side, "if you want, my home is always available to you. I know you loved the bath."

Groaning, Emma held up her hand. "Don't remind me! I'm a bathtub baby. I hate showers."

"Then," Khalid said, his voice low and smoky, "perhaps once a week you will consider coming to take advantage of the bath in my home?"

Emma managed a polite smile. "I don't think

so, Captain Shaheen. It wouldn't look proper to the military. Thank you, though, for the offer." Emma couldn't afford to make him angry at her. Yet, she was walking the edge of the sword with this very available male pilot who was interested in her.

"Pity," he remarked. "Well, then I will fly the CH-47 back to Bagram alone. I will miss you, Captain Cantrell."

"Oh," Emma said lightly, standing and picking up her helmet bag, "I think you'll have plenty to keep you busy, Captain Shaheen."

Back at her tent, Emma threw her helmet bag on her cot. She turned to sit down in the camp chair at her desk. Upset with herself, she decided that she was too easily swayed by Khalid, for whatever reason.

Tomorrow morning, he'd fly in at dawn with another load of boxes for the village of Zor Barawul. They would continue this pace daily or every other day, depending upon the distance involved.

"Hey, Emma!"

Emma turned toward the open flaps of her tent. Nike Alexander poked her head in. "Nike, come on in! How are you?"

The BJS woman pilot slipped in, threw her helmet bag next to Emma's on the cot and sat down in the extra chair. "Okay. Just got off a hot fire fight around Zor Barawul. We kicked ass. How are you? I haven't had time to catch up with you lately. What's happening?"

"Just delivered our first boxes of books to Do Bandi. I had lunch at the chow hall and was coming back here to drop off my helmet and then go to the BJS HQ to fill out my report." Emma watched as Nike pushed the black curls off her sweaty brow. She saw the armpits of her flight suit were wet with perspiration. Flying an Apache in a fire fight made the adrenaline rocket upward. She saw pink spots on Nike's olive-skinned cheeks. Her friend was still caught up in the adrenaline charge from the fire fight.

"Was that your boss I just passed out there?" Nike hooked a thumb toward the tent opening. "That eye candy that's long and lean? Black hair? Blue eyes?"

Groaning, Emma nodded. "Yes, that's Captain Khalid Shaheen."

Nike gave her a wicked look. "Hey, if I hadn't met the man of my dreams recently, I'd definitely give that dude a second look. He's absolutely handsome."

Sighing, Emma gave her friend a dirty look. "Don't make this any worse than it is, Nike. Think about me. I have to work with the guy for the next six months and remain immune to him."

Laughing, Nike slapped her knee. "Oh, Emma! You're single. You're not involved with anyone. Why wouldn't you think about getting hooked up with him?"

Emma explained all the details to Nike about Brody Parker. As she did, she watched her friend become more serious. At the end of her explanation, she watched the excitement die in Nike's eyes. "So you see, I need a good recommendation from Captain Shaheen for my personnel jacket. I have to dig myself out of the black eye I gave us," she said, desperate. Opening her hands, Emma added, "And I don't dare let him know I like him, Nike. I fight it constantly. But I'm afraid he's just another player in disguise."

"I see," Nike muttered, sitting up, hands on her knees. "I'm hoping in my own way to overcome our mistake, too. But at least I don't have to worry about falling in love with my boss. That's an extra added strain on you."

"I'm not falling in love with him," Emma said more sharply than she'd intended. "I like the guy, yes. But love? No."

"Hmm," Nike murmured, a grin pulling at her

lips, "sure don't look like it from my end. Every time you talked about him, your voice went soft and your eyes got that faraway, dreamy look."

Emma stood up, scowling at her best friend. "Nike, you're wrong."

Nike stood, laughed and picked up her helmet bag. "Okay, then prove it."

Chapter 6

"When does Shaheen arrive at Zor Barawul?" Asad Malik demanded. He sat crouched in front of a small fire, warming his hands. The cave where he and his men hid sat across from the Afghan village, which was perched on top of a hill.

Merzad, a trusted warrior, stood attentively by the Taliban leader. "My lord, our spy in the village told our man that next week Captain Shaheen, his sister Kinah and an American woman pilot are to fly educational books and desks into this village."

Scowling, Malik took a tin cup filled with steaming chai from the cook, Omald. He looked across the fire as the boy fed the fifteen men under his command. Omald was only thirteen, an orphan Malik had taken under his wing. He had been ten when Malik had found him in a burned-out border village. He had brainwashed the child and turned him into his personal servant. Omald's job was to make him chai, feed him, take care of his horse and serve his soldiers whatever scant food they could steal.

"Do you think that they will arrive with an Apache escort?" Merzad asked, taking a proffered cup of chai from Omald.

Shrugging, Malik enjoyed the warmth of the fire. The cave was dry and cold. Outside, April rain fell. There was a gray pall over the entire area and Zor Barawul was hidden in the mists and cold mountain air. "I hope not. We never know," he muttered, stroking his black-and-gray beard. At fifty, the harshness of his life as a leader in the Taliban, was catching up with Malik. His joints ached in the winter snows and it worsened during the spring rains. Now, he looked forward to the summer heat when his arthritis stopped bothering him as much.

Merzad crouched down next to him, his narrow face set in a deep scowl. The black beard on his face was fuzzy and unkempt. All the men smelled. They went days, even weeks, without a place to clean themselves up or comb their beards and hair. He looked over at his beloved leader, a giant of a man with broad shoulders, a deep chest and powerful, sun-darkened hands covered with scars. Merzad felt a brotherly love for his fellow Pakistani. They'd grown up in the same village, survived terrible odds and gone on to carry the jihad into Afghanistan. Like Malik, Merzad felt strongly that the Taliban needed to be back in control of the country before the U.N. came in with troops to "free" the people from them.

Continuing to stroke the beard that fell nearly to his chest, Malik murmured to his best friend, "I hope to fulfill my promise to Shaheen and his sister. I killed Shaheen's fiancée two years ago. I've waited patiently, praying daily to Allah to give me another chance to kill him and his infidel sister. We were blessed when we hit the base camp to spot Shaheen there. Our spies have kept good track of him since then."

"They are both infidels," Merzad muttered. "They might be born to a Muslim father, but he's a Sufi." The word *Sufi* came out like a growling curse from the lean forty-five-year-old soldier.

Snorting, Malik sipped the delicious cinnamon-sprinkled chai. "Sufis are our enemies," he acknowledged. "I have no use for mystics of any kind." He smiled, remembering his rapes of Najela. She had fought him, and, to this day, he bore four fingernail marks on his right cheek where she'd clawed at him. No matter, he'd had his way with her. His loins warmed to the memory of taking the feisty black-haired beauty. She'd fought every time and Malik had enjoyed the encounters. Finally, he'd grown bored with her bravery and had slit her throat as she slept. They'd thrown her body into a village where he knew his archenemy, Khalid Shaheen, would find her. Again, his lips twitched with those fond memories. He anticipated capturing Kinah. She was fiery and gave no quarter. Malik, in his own way, admired the Sufi woman, but his hatred was even more intense toward her than it had been toward Najela.

"According to our source," Merzad said, pleased, "you will have them all coming to Zor Barawul."

"Yes," he muttered, "but the leader of that village is pro-American. His village, over the last year, has been protected by A-teams, given

medical and dental care from the Americans."
Shaking his head, he said, "We must be careful
here, Merzad. We can't just openly walk into
their village and threaten them as we used to.
We tried that just this week and got nowhere.
I've lost half of my men to the Apaches. We
must rethink and try a different strategy."

Agreeing, Merzad sipped his chai, deep in
thought. "It used to be easy to come across the
border and threaten the leaders of these villages.
Now, this past year, they have received all kinds
of aid from the U.N., the U.S. Army and charity
organizations from around the world. They no
longer fear us." His mouth dipped downward as
did his thin black brows.

"They will fear us again," Malik muttered,
finishing off his chai and handing the cup back
to his servant. He slowly rose on painful knees
and rearranged the two bandoliers of ammunition across his chest. Looking around the large,
dry cave, he saw that his men had bedded down

and were sleeping, their rifles next to them. They'd just suffered a terrible defeat at the hands of the American Apache helicopters. The best thing to do, Malik knew, was to let them heal and lick their wounds, give them hot food and chai to rebuild their confidence. He silently cursed the combat helicopters. They were the bane of his existence. His mind spun with possible plans.

Zor Barawul was considered an American stronghold now. Malik could recall when he had owned that village. The old, crippled leaders cowered before him as he rode through like a conquering hero, his men following him. *No longer.* Allah would show him a way to infiltrate the village. His whole focus was on capturing or killing Khalid and Kinah Shaheen. Then his revenge would be complete.

After ordering another cup of chai, he watched the young lad quickly pour it from the tea kettle across the grate of the fire. Malik took it and scowled. The Shaheens were infidels. They weren't even full-blooded Afghans. The blood of the Irish ran through their veins. Malik hadn't liked it when the Shaheens began to come regularly to the villages along the border. First, it was the elder Shaheen who had thrown his money at the villagers. Malik cursed the Sufi. All of them were stupid dreamers who thought love could solve the world's problems. How wrong they were! All of the money the elder Shaheen had given the villages had created schools. Malik had been livid with rage when he'd found out that girls were being taught, and he'd come in and destroyed every one of those schools.

Of all things! Malik was enraged to find out that five years later, the stupid girls were going to be educated once more by the Shaheen son and daughter. What an utter waste of time! A donkey was far more valuable than an accursed woman! Women had little value except as brood mares to bear a man's children and further the male family line. *Stupid women! Women must know their place. I will show them, once and for all. Once I capture Kinah Shaheen I will use her and kill her. Once she's dead, I will dump her body in Zor Barawul and let the women there see what will happen to them if they so much as pick up a book.*

Emma moaned. She turned over in her cot, the layers of blankets keeping her warm. Khalid was with her in her dream. He was touching her cheek lingeringly. She could feel the roughness of his fingers as they curved and followed her cheekbone. The look in his blue eyes, hooded with intent, reminded Emma of a summer thunderstorm. Skin tingling wildly in the wake of his slow caress, Emma sighed and leaned forward. She was naked and so was he. They knelt in front of one another on a sunny, grassy slope. She didn't know where they were, only that it was warm, beautiful and the fragrance of roses surrounded them.

"You are my beloved rose with freckles," Khalid murmured, watching her cheeks turn pink as he whispered the words. "The sun may rise and set, but the rays of love emanate from your heart to mine."

As her breasts brushed his dark, hairy chest, they tightened and a deep throb began in her lower body. Oh, how Emma wanted his hand to trail downward, hold and caress her taut breasts. A softened sigh slipped from between her lips. Khalid smiled into her eyes.

"You are the rose who grows in my heart, beloved."

Her mind was starting to come unhinged as his fingers trailed across her eyebrow, down her temple and back to her cheek. "Rumi…was that Rumi?" she managed in a whisper.

His smile increased. "Rumi talks of the rose. Do his words not touch your heart, also?"

Nodding, Emma moved her hands up across his shoulders. She felt the warmth of the sun upon them. Khalid was so strong and steady, as if he knew who he was and where he was going in his life. Emma wished she felt that way. Confidence radiated from him like the sun itself. As she absorbed a sense of protection and love from him, Emma's lids shuttered closed. His fingers outlined her lips and she wanted to kiss him.

"No yet, beloved. Allow my hands to remember every inch of your beautiful being. My heart needs to map you, remember you and breathe you into itself...."

Heat throbbed through her womanly core. Fingers digging into the hard flesh of his shoulders, Emma whimpered his name, begging him to kiss her. She was not disappointed. As Khalid's strong mouth brushed her lips, she trembled. She felt him smiling against her. She smiled in return. With her eyes closed, Emma simply wanted to feel the texture of his mouth, the heat of his ragged breath whispering across her cheek, the male fragrance that was only him.

She opened her lips and pressed into his smiling mouth. They slid and melted together as if in a slow-motion dance of fusion. Emma realized in some far corner of her barely functioning mind that Khalid was courting her slowly, enjoying her with a thoroughness she'd never experienced before. There was no hurry. No rush. Just…timelessness and being rocked and cradled with his mouth sliding upon hers. There was such strength and yet incredible tenderness as he asked her to open her mouth more so that he could take her fully into himself.

Had she ever been kissed like this? No. Every sip of his lips upon hers sent wild tingles down to her breasts and fueled the need to take him completely within her. Khalid's slow exploration of her lips now moved to her cheeks. His mouth scorched a path of neediness with each caress upon her skin. He traced the outline of her brows with his lips. Soft, rose-petal touches grazed her closed eyelids. Strands of hair caught beneath his seeking mouth as he lingered on each of her delicate ears. Emma surrendered to the slow, delicious seduction by Khalid.

"You are honey, my sweet, sweet woman," he whispered into her right ear. Moving his fingers upward from her jaw, Khalid framed her face and pulled back just enough to drown in her dark-green eyes that were sultry with need—of him. "The sweetness of your heart bathes my wounded heart. Honey heals. The sugar of life nurtures new bees into being born and birthing. You are no different…." He trailed a series of kisses from her brow down to her parted lips. There, he halted and barely grazed them with his own. "And like the bees, the honey of your heart allows me to be reborn anew…."

"Emma! Wake up!"

Emma jerked into a sitting position, completely disoriented.

"Over here!" Nike called, her head sticking through the opening in the tent. "Wake up!"

"Oh," Emma gasped. "What time is it?" Khalid's words and fiery, evocative touches were real. Her body throbbed and ached. Embarrassed that Nike had had to awaken her, she looked at her watch.

"Oh, God," Emma groaned, "I'm late!!"

"No kidding," Nike said. "What's the matter? You having a sexy dream about Khalid?"

Emma leaped out of bed and fumbled for her flight boots beneath the cot. Shocked at Nike's intuitiveness, Emma muttered, "Oh, forget it, Nike! I was up late last night writing reports, that's all."

Nike grinned. "Oh, sure. Well, hey, Khalid's on the tarmac waiting for you."

"Okay, okay." Pulling out her boots, Emma

twisted around. "Can you tell him I'll be there in ten minutes?"

Laughing, Nike said, "Yeah, no problem. Was it a good dream?"

Emma glared at her. Nike chortled and disappeared. How could her girlfriend know about that wonderful dream? Stymied, Emma tore her mind from that to getting dressed, getting to the toilet and grabbing her flight bag. She was late! She'd never slept through the alarm on the bedstand! Ever. Grabbing the clock, Emma realized with a sinking feeling that the alarm was on, but she hadn't heard it.

With a moan of trepidation, Emma hurried to make up for lost time.

Emma was breathless as she arrived at Ops. As usual, it was a beehive of nonstop activity, planes and helos landing and taking off in an invisible dance known only to air-control-tower personnel. She saw Khalid leaning against the fender of the Apache, reading a book. He was relaxed, his head bent down, his helmet bag sitting next to him on the skirt of the helo. The April day was cloudy and chilly. It had rained all night. Puddles lay everywhere on the asphalt landing strip. Ragged, scudding clouds hid the mountains that surrounded the base camp.

Sucking in a breath, Emma walked quickly toward Khalid, her flight boots splashing through several puddles. She saw him lift his head. Instantly, her heart rate doubled. Why did he have to be so handsome? Just looking at the man, who was all warrior and yet so incredibly sensitive, made her feel even more breathless than the run from the tent to Ops had. Emma girded herself for his censure.

"Good morning," Khalid greeted, giving her a warm and appreciative look. "Nike said you overslept."

"I did." Emma pushed several strands of hair off her face. "I'm sorry. I set my alarm but I slept right through it. That's never happened before."

Khalid saw how upset Emma was, her cheeks stained with heat. It only made her freckles more obvious and gave her a decidedly girlish look, at variance with the competent combat pilot she was. "Relax," he urged quietly. "We are in no rush. The weather is bad and we are going to have to wait for the clouds to rise more before we can fly nap-of-the-earth." CH-47s did not have all-terrain radar to see where they were going, and flying a hundred feet off the ground required a good set of eyes and no fog or low-hanging clouds obscuring the terrain.

"Oh," Emma said, relieved, "that's good news."

"Here," he said, handing her the book, "this is a gift for you. I realize it's not military protocol, but I would like to share my world with you a little bit. Take it. We'll go to the chow hall and get some chai and wait until the clouds lift." He picked up his helmet bag.

Emma looked down at the book. She nearly dropped it. It was a paperback called *Rumi: In the Arms of the Beloved*. Stunned, she looked up at Khalid.

"How did you know?" she croaked, confused as she held the book. How could he know about her torrid dream of this morning? Was it all over the internet? Nike had known too. Now, Khalid, of all things! Emma stood there feeling stupid for a moment. She stared at the cover. It showed several men in tall, red, Turkish caps wearing white clothing and whirling around in long skirts. Because of her one-year saturation into Pashto, Emma realized these were Sufi whirling dervishes. They would whirl around and around to music and it allowed them to go into a mystical trance to connect with the Beloved, a direct connection with God.

"Know what?" Khalid asked, confused, as

he walked at her side. Emma's brow wrinkled. There was shock in her green eyes. She kept turning the book over and over, as if it were too hot to handle. Khalid wondered if he'd over-stepped her personal bounds again. Was giving her a book such a crime in the military's mind-set? After all, they were both captains, of equal rank. He saw no reason to think a book was too personal a gift. But, judging from the rush of redness to Emma's cheeks, the way she tucked her lower lip between her teeth, maybe it was.

Gripping the book, Emma muttered, "Oh, nothing. I'm still waking up." She hoped the excuse would sail with Khalid. It did. The worry dissolved from his handsome features. And then, abruptly, she said, "Thank you. This was a very nice gift." They were love poems! Inwardly, Emma felt as if Khalid could see straight through her, to her heart, and was fully aware of the throbbing ache that still lingered in her lower body. His eyes at times made her think he truly had paranormal abilities. Had his intuition whispered to bring her a book of love poems because, somehow, he knew how she felt? Emma always felt out of step in Khalid's presence. He thrilled her, mesmerized her, made her want him in every way possible. And he was off-limits to her for a damned good reason. Emma wasn't ready to toss her wounded heart into any relationship yet.

"Ah, yes. Well, a good, bracing cup of delicious chai will cure your sleepiness," Khalid chuckled. They made their way through muddy ruts, leaping over puddles and walking around the larger ones.

Emma glanced at her watch. It was barely 0800. The chow hall would be packed, the noise high and it was the last place she wanted to be. Right now, she felt terribly vulnerable. Was it the dream? Or something more? Emma swore she still felt every touch of Khalid, her skin still retaining memory of it. "Sounds good," she managed, her voice sounding strangled even to her.

To her relief, Khalid found an empty table in a far corner. She sat down with the book on the table and watched him thread through the men and women to get to where the Afghan widow sold the chai. Khalid had such grace. He walked with pride and almost always had a smile lurking at the corners of his sensual mouth. Fumbling with the book, Emma finally opened it. She began to read some of the poems. Instantly, heat nettled her cheeks and she slapped the book shut and pushed it away, as if would incriminate her. The memory of that very real dream was still too close, too evocative. Reading Rumi's poems was like fanning the fires of her desire once more.

Emma shook her head. Somehow, and God only knew how, she had to erase Khalid from her body and her yearning heart. But how? Emma couldn't blame Khalid for how her body was behaving. Did he know that casual smile of his just made her ache to grab him and haul him into her bed? Emma was sure he'd be shocked by her very brazen instincts. Khalid was gentleman, a throwback to another century where a man smoothly courted a woman with flowers, gifts, looks and compliments without ever touching her.

Sighing, she rubbed her face with her hands. What made her situation worse was that Emma wanted to be in Khalid's world. It was more than just sex. The mystery of the man himself compelled her. Not that he hid any aspect of himself, but her curiosity went much deeper. If Emma was honest with herself, she wanted to hear every thought Khalid had. What were his growing-up years like? How was he able to adjust to American life? What adventures had he had in the U.S. Army while learning how to fly the Apache? And how could a Sufi be a warrior? There was so much Emma wanted to know. And it was all personal. She spotted Khalid coming back, moving as quietly as fog around groups of people coming and going from the chow hall. In his hands, Khalid held two cups of chai.

Emma felt as if she were sitting on a volcano about to erupt. As Khalid handed her the chai and sat down opposite her, Emma did all she could to ignore her attraction.

"The chai will help you wake up," he observed wryly, lifting his cup in toast.

His teasing eased her anxiety. "Salud," she muttered, clinking the rim of his cup.

Khalid sat with his elbows on the table. "Have you looked at Rumi's book yet?"

"No," Emma lied. She didn't want to get on the topic of love with him. That would be like holding a grenade with the pin released from it. "These are whirling dervishes on the cover, aren't they?" Emma hoped this safe conversation would steer him away from the main topic of the book.

"Ah yes, the young men who spend years learning how to turn in a circle, remain grounded and yet, open their hearts to Allah." Khalid smiled. "They are the role models for the rest of us. I have seen some twirl for an hour or more without stopping."

Emma drank her chai, relieved the conversation was on religion and not her. "That's an amazing feat in and of itself. I couldn't twirl in a circle for probably more than thirty seconds before losing my balance and falling down."

Chuckling, Khalid said, "At one time, I begged my father to send me to a Sufi learning center. From childhood on I had seen the whirling dervishes at the festivals. They were magical! I remember standing in front of my father, his hands on my shoulders, and my eyes were huge as they whirled past us like tornados."

Emma sipped more of her chai. "I can just see

you as a little kid: all eyes. That would be an incredible thing to experience." Emma recalled the magic carpet and genies of the *Arabian Nights*, and felt those myths were still alive— between them, for whatever reason. The magic seemed to leap to life every time they talked to one another. And now, she'd dropped their conversation to the personal level. Groaning inwardly, she felt trapped.

Khalid drowned in Emma's warm forest-green gaze. "Yes, I fell in love with the mystical segment of our Sufi way of life. My father gently turned me away from becoming a dervish."

"Do you regret that?"

"No. In reality, my father saw I was not ready for such schooling. I was a very adventurous boy given to taking risks and boldly exploring where few ever went." His smile increased. "He knew my love of flying. I thought as a child I could fly in the invisible ethers that the whirling dervishes flew on. My father was far more practical. He harnessed my love of flying with military service with the U.S. Army. I hadn't thought of that path, but it felt like the right one for me." He pointed his index finger upward. "When I'm flying, I feel like the dervishes, held in the invisible mystical hands of the universe. There's nothing quite like it."

"I agree," Emma said. "The sky takes away all my fears, worries and anxieties about the future."

"Hmm, perhaps we're both eagles of the Kush, eh?" he teased.

Emma laughed, and the words flew out of her mouth, "Oh no, you're a snow leopard! No doubt about that." And then, she gulped, set her mug down and realized her gaffe. Amusement glimmered in Khalid's expression.

"Indeed. You see me as a beautiful and rare snow leopard?"

Emma froze. No matter what she'd say, she

would incriminate herself. *Damn!* Her heart sank into her boots. What had she just done? Was she so exhausted that she was unable to erect her defenses, keep the conversation strictly focused on their mission?

Khalid leaned forward, his voice dropping to an intimate whisper. "I often wondered how you really saw me, Captain Emma Cantrell. Snow leopards are perhaps the most beautiful and rarest of cats in the world. There are only a handful who live in the Kush. I was fortunate enough to see one, once. His coat was of soft gray-white with spots of brown that matched the mountain slope. He blended in so well that at first I did not spot him. But my friend, who was a biologist, did. I watched that cat move from one side of the rocky, unstable slope to the other. He had such feline grace, such quiet power and authority, all I could do was stare with admiration at him." Khalid sat up and gave her a dazzling smile. "So, you see me as a snow leopard. What a wonderful compliment. Thank you!" There was no question; his heart was opening to Emma.

Chapter 7

When they landed at Zor Barawul, the April showers had eased up. It was almost noon when Emma powered down the CH-47 and shut off the engines. The village was a hub of activity. Two days earlier, it had been under attack by the Taliban. Now two A-teams were present. One was stationed on an outpost that overlooked the valley where Zor Barawul sat. The other team lived in the village itself.

It seemed nothing could dampen Khalid's spirits. He unhooked the jack from his helmet,

pulled it off his head and seemed utterly un-
affected by the violence that surrounded them.
Emma marveled at that, but she figured, as her
hands flew over the controls, that his Sufi perspective gave him that sense of protection.

The rains of April made the village a sea of
mud. Warm in her thick nylon jacket and glad
to be wearing it, Emma heard the ramp grinding down. On this particular flight, they had
brought a dentist and a dental hygienist from
Bagram. Emma wasn't happy about keeping
the CH-47 on the ground all day, considering
the recent attacks. Too often, if a bird stayed on
the ground, the Taliban would sneak up and lob
mortars at it. However, they'd be staying to help
out and, near sunset, they'd fly the army dental
team back to Bagram.

Turning in her seat, Emma stood up and saw
her load master, Sgt. Steve Bailey unhooking
his harness. The twenty-two-year old blond was
tall and gangly. When Khalid walked back to

help him organize the boxes to be off-loaded, she thought they looked like brothers body-wise. As always, Emma remained alert and on guard. She swept her gaze around the area where the helo was sitting. It was parked on the tip of the hill. There was a fifty-foot diameter landing area. The rocky slopes dropped off steeply to a valley a thousand feet below them.

Khalid eased between the cargo boxes. They were battened down with sturdy netting and nylon straps that kept the boxes from flying all over while they were in the air. He saw Abbas, a tall older village leader with a deeply lined, narrow face waiting for him near the ramp. He wore a dark-gold wool turban, a gray robe and wool cloak over his proud shoulders. His black and gray beard was neatly trimmed, his eyebrows straight and thick across his dark-brown eyes.

Emma smiled to herself as Abbas shook Khalid's hand, pumping it up and down. The leader then leaned forward and kissed the pilot on each cheek. This was a common Afghan custom and a sign of friendship. She heard Khalid murmur, *"As-salaam alaikum."*

Abbas returned the warm greeting with *"Wa alaikum as-salaam wa rahmatu Allah,"* in return. That meant "And to you be peace together with God's mercy."

Emma liked the sincere greeting. Khalid had already prepped her for the important people who ran this village. At Abbas's side was his wife, Jameela. She was dressed in a black burka, only her cinnamon-brown eyes looking out through the cross-hatched material. Jameela had been college-educated in Pakistan and spoke fluent English. At her side was Ateefa, their daughter.

Emma felt her heart contract with pain at the sight of the five-year-old girl with a prosthesis on her right leg. Her black hair was clean, brushed and hung around her small shoulders.

There were shoes on her feet. Emma knew most children in these border villages went barefoot all year long, even in the harsh, icy winters and cold, rainy springtime. Today, as she pulled the green scarf from the thigh pocket on her flight suit, Emma smiled to herself. A gaggle of wide-eyed, curious children of all ages peeked around the adults huddled near the last mud hut at the end of the village. They too had shoes. Not only that, they were dressed warmly in clothes that had been donated by Americans. Emma knew a lot had been done for this village and the people were grateful.

Placing the scarf around her head, Emma walked down the ramp. The A-team helped bring the boxes out of the cargo hold of the helo. Several wooden pallets had been set up by Bailey where the boxes would be placed. That way, the boxes remained dry and protected from the mud. There was an air of excitement, as if a festival were in progress. The U.S. Army dental team, consisting of two men, forged ahead of Emma. They would give their greetings to Abbas and then get on with their work. A dental hut had long ago been set up and they came in monthly to help the villagers.

Emma waited to present herself to Abbas. When she was next, she murmured the same greeting, her hand pressed to her heart and giving Abbas a slight bow, a sign of respect. He'd never met her before and official salutations were a must.

Abbas thrust his hand out to her. *"Salaam,"* Emma said, as he shook her hand, warmth dancing in his dark eyes. He then leaned down and brushed a kiss on each of her cheeks. His beard tickled her. She returned the greeting and then stepped back. Her ability to speak Pashto to him made his eyes light up with surprise.

"Ah, you speak our language, Captain. That is an unexpected gift."

Emma smiled. "I'm working with Captain

Shaheen and his sister Kinah for the next six months. He asked for someone who could speak Pashto. It makes it easier on everyone."

Abbas looked over at his wife. "Indeed, it does. Please, this is my beloved wife, Jameela. She will take you to our home where you will share a cup of hot chai with her. As I understand it, the desks for the children's school have arrived today. Perhaps you two can decide where they need to be set up? I will have my men take them out of the boxes and assemble them."

Emma nodded. "As you like, my lord. I'm here to serve." She saw the old man's expression soften and seemed grateful for their presence. Khalid had told her that Abbas was highly educated and had a degree in biology. He'd received university training in Pakistan and returned to the village of his birth. He had been responsible for breeding better animals, improving sheep's fleece and his progressive leadership had influenced a number of other border villages. The man was courageous in Emma's eyes. He had fought against the Taliban, but had caved to their demands when his people's lives were threatened. Now, with over a year's worth of U.S. Army protection and help, this village has flourished.

Jameela stepped forward and shook Emma's hand. "Welcome, Captain Cantrell. I'm so thrilled you are here with us. I am Jameela."

Smiling, Emma shook her hand. They traded kisses on the cheeks. Jameela brought her daughter forward. "And this is Ateefa, our youngest. Her leg was destroyed by a mine when she was three years old. Last year, thanks to Captain Gavin Jackson, a prosthesis was made for Ateefa. And look at her today! She has thrown her crutches away and can run and race with all her friends."

Emma crouched down and took Ateefa's small hand. The little girl was beautiful, with large black eyes and a sweet smile. "How do you do, Ateefa? I'm glad you have a leg to run around on now. How are you getting along with it?"

"Fine, soldier lady," Ateefa said shyly, putting her fingers in her mouth.

Emma chuckled. "You have a beautiful daughter."

Abbas touched his wife's shoulder. "Beautiful children from my beautiful wife. Go, Jameela. Take our guest and allow her to warm up in our house."

"Of course, my dearest husband," Jameela said. She held out her hand to Emma. "Come. This is an exciting day for all of us. The children have been longing to see their new desks. After some chai, I'll take you over to the house we have chosen to become our school for our children."

The excitement was palpable as Emma walked at Jameela's side. Ateefa and several other young children raced ahead. The main street had deep ruts created by the donkeys who pulled the carts. It seemed everyone was out to greet them. Emma felt her heart lift. This is what life was really about: helping those who had less than she did. She followed Jameela to a beautiful two-story stone building with a red wooden door. It was the only home that had two stories. All the rest were made of adobe mud bricks, or, for those who could afford it, built from stone.

Looking over her shoulder, Emma noticed Khalid with a heavy box balanced on one shoulder, leading the A-team down the street with their own boxes of desks. A number of children across the street stood at the opened door of what would become their school. They were like excited little puppies wriggling around, giggling, excitement shining in their faces. Emma smiled. It was a great day for Zor Barawul. Still, she felt tense. She sensed that the Taliban was nearby monitoring them and this sent a chill up Emma's spine as she entered the warm home.

Asad Malik watched the activity at Zor Barawul through a set of Russian binoculars. The beat-up set had served him well over the years. He'd killed a Russian officer with his pistol and divested him of anything of value, including his binoculars. It reminded Malik of their victory over the Russians who had tried to tame the wild Afghan people. They hadn't succeeded, and if he had anything to do with it, the Americans and the U.N. would leave with their tails tucked between their legs, too.

"What do we do?" Merzad asked as he stood near the opening of the cave looking across the valley to Zor Barawul.

"Nothing," Malik murmured. "Not yet…"

Frowning, Merzad offered, "You know, we have two new boys, orphans, with us. Why not send them into the village as our spies? Let them pretend to be hungry and lost. Someone will surely help them. With all the food, money and medical gifts old Abbas has gotten in the last year, they will take in our 'lost' boys. They could become our eyes and ears, Lord Malik."

The plan wasn't a bad one. Malik dropped the binoculars back on his chest. Turning, he nodded. "That's a good plan. Our only problem is we haven't had either boy long enough to brainwash them properly. What if they run away and side with Abbas? What then?"

Merzad shrugged. "When you rescued them three months ago, they were starving. They've been treated with nothing but discipline, been given food, a blanket and I believe they can be our spies without concern."

Rubbing his beard, Malik glanced over his shoulder. Both boys were sitting near the fire, recently fed and cleaning some of the weapons for his soldiers. Their jobs were to clean weapons, help the cook, water the horses and do the bidding of his soldiers. Soon, they would be taught how to fire the weapons. For now, cleaning a rifle was crucial because it taught them about the weapons and it gave them prestige within the group. Being trusted to handle such weapons earned them respect from his soldiers. The boys desired to be a part of his family.

"Benham is thirteen. He's got the slowness of a donkey pulling a cart, though."

"Agreed," Merzad said in a low voice so no one could overhear them. "He's slow but very loyal to us."

Malik's gaze moved to the ten-year-old boy crouched nearby with a partly dismantled AK-47 on a thin, tattered blanket before him. "Fahran is the smart one." The scrawny child wore a dark-blue woolen robe, his feet bare and sticking out from beneath the dirtied material. He had black hair, startling green eyes and he reminded Malik of a wily fox.

"You have doubts about Fahran?" Merzad

probed. "When you say nothing but you look for a long time, I know there are problems you are contemplating."

Malik gave his compatriot an appreciative glance. Merzad was forty-five years old and his best friend. Having been born in the same village gave them a bonding like no other. Merzad had saved his life a number of times and vice versa. Malik trusted few, but Merzad had earned his trust. "I'm unsure about him, that's all. He's very young."

"But alert and smart," Merzad offered. "He's learned how to take apart an AK-47 and put it back together as no one we've ever seen. Even now, he instructs Benham on the next step. That older boy has been at it as long as he, but Benham stumbles and is forgetful."

"Mmm," Malik said, hand on his beard, studying the two youths near the fire. "The real question is: do I trust Fahran on such a spy mission?"

Saying nothing, Merzad stood quietly. He knew better than to argue Malik in or out of anything.

"Benham comes from a farm-laborer background," Malik said, talking to himself. "He has no education whatsoever. Our men are teaching him to read by learning the Koran. Fahran has been schooled and comes from a well-educated family in his village. He reads, writes and speaks several dialects already."

"Do you think he knows English?"

"How could he?" Malik said, looking over at his friend. "He comes from an Afghan border village in the north. According to him, his parents took their schooling in Pakistan. No, I doubt very seriously if he knows English."

"If you are considering him for this mission, I can ask him," Merzad suggested. "If he does, that would be a strong reason to have him go. He could eavesdrop on the Americans. They'd never suspect someone like him would know English, much less understand it."

Nodding, Malik said, "Have one of our men ask him. Then, let me know."

"Of course," Merzad said, leaving his side.

Malik turned and placed the binoculars to his eyes once more. How badly he wanted to sneak over under the cover of night and lob a rocket or mortar round into that helo. Chances were that it would lift off before dark. They rarely left any helicopter on the ground overnight.

His mind turned back to the ten-year-old Afghan orphan, Fahran. Malik didn't fully trust anyone that smart. His loyal soldiers could read the Koran but few knew how to write. He wanted to keep them dumb. It suited his purpose. Merzad, of course, knew how to read, could write and spoke a number of different dialects, but Malik trusted him.

The boy with the bright-green eyes, his black hair straight and shaggy around his head, was quick and agile. His small, greasy fingers flew over the weapon with knowing ease. Malik had entered a village one night where his men had killed a number of Sufi families. One of his soldiers found Fahran hidden beneath a bed, shivering like a dog. They'd dragged him out, kidnapped him and brought him along with them because they needed young boys for their unit. Benham had been found in shock, wandering around outside the village, crying for his parents, who had been killed.

At first, Malik recalled, Fahran had tried to run away several times, and each time, he was caught. Finally, the soldiers kept a rope tied around his thin ankle. If Fahran tried to escape, the rope would tug in the soldier's sleeping hand and awaken him. Fahran had tried it once and was whipped soundly, his back bleeding from ten lashes. After that, Fahran seemed to accept his fate. But had he really surrendered? Malik didn't know and wished mightily that he had the answer to that question.

With a sigh, he returned to watching the activity across the valley. Merzad would find out if the boy knew English. For Malik, that would seal the deal one way or another.

"Look! Look!" Ateefa cried, sitting down at the first assembled desk. She beamed with excitement at her parents who stood in the large, cold room smiling down at her with pride. All around her men were tearing open boxes and everyone was assembling the wooden desks. Children were barely able to stand still as they waited to be assigned a desk by Jameela.

Emma stood near the wife of the leader, smiling. There was an air of celebration, the room filled with men, the laughter of children and as many families who could squeeze in to watch the miraculous event. She thought about American children who took a school desk for granted. Much of the world did not possess the riches of America, and watching Khalid and the A-team work to assemble the desks made Emma's heart warm with pride.

Jameela joined the wives of the other children and asked them to open several boxes that held crayons, notebook paper, pens, pencils, rulers and erasers. The small group of younger women eagerly descended upon the huge box, glad to be part of the activity. Immediately, all their children gathered around the boxes, touching the cardboard and anxious to see what was inside.

Emma couldn't help the men with the desks, although she wanted to. That was considered a man's job, not a woman's. Several more A-team members set up the newly assembled desks. Others hauled away the cardboard and placed it in neat rows in front of a huge green chalkboard that had been hung in place earlier in the morning.

She saw the joy in Khalid's ruddy features as he crouched and gathered the pieces to assemble another desk. Emma didn't want to feel so good about watching him. His long fingers moved with an assuredness and precision that made her crave his touch. She couldn't erase the haunting dream of him courting her, kissing her. Every time his gaze met hers, she quickly averted her eyes so that he couldn't, somehow, read what was in her thoughts and heart. What to do? This wasn't getting any easier, Emma realized with a sinking feeling.

Of course, it didn't help that she was drawn to the man who read love poems by Rumi, either. In her foreign language class she had read his poems, and she understood why Khalid was a devout reader of his work. The ancient mystic touched her heart and soul as well. Who wouldn't be touched by this man's greater awareness of the human condition, his acceptance of the fact that no one was perfect, and yet that we all deserve another chance? Emma liked Rumi a lot, but she wasn't about to confide that to Khalid since it would make their relationship that much more personal. Right now, she had enough to juggle emotionally about the Afghan pilot.

Emma watched as several children mimicked the A-team members by helping them haul the cardboard out of the classroom. It wouldn't be wasted. The cardboard would be taken to a barn for future use by the villagers. The mountains in this area had a lot of brush and very few trees. Wood was hard to come by. The cardboard would be a welcome fire starter in the mornings around here, Emma realized.

Khalid set up another desk. As they were put into working order, Jameela announced the name of the next child to be assigned that seat. Emma watched the pride and excitement in the eyes of the children, and the hope mirrored in the faces of the proud parents. Her heart opened to Khalid, who dusted off his hands and walked toward them. Kinah had the supply box. She handed out all the items to the parents, who in turn, gave them to their children. Truly, Khalid and his sister were changing the world one child, one village at a time.

The warmth in his sparkling blue eyes stole Emma's breath for a moment. It was a fierce, burning look Khalid gave only to her and it made her feel so special. Blessed by her lover's gaze, as Rumi would say. Khalid moved over the cardboard debris to reach Abbas's side. How shaky she felt after that hooded look that had lasted only a fraction of a second between them. Emma tried to ignore it.

If only she could find something to dislike about Khalid and focus on that. He was terribly human, but as for a real flaw? She couldn't detect one—yet. It could be the one thing to protect herself from wanting a personal relationship with him. The more she worked with Khalid, the more Brody Parker dissolved into her past.

Chapter 8

"Come," Khalid entreated Emma as she stood near the edge of the village. The sun had just set and the grayish dusk was upon them. "Let's give the sergeant relief from staying with our CH-47. He needs to eat before we leave."

Emma hadn't seen Khalid the rest of the day. The men had been busy over at the schoolroom, and she'd been with the women and school supplies at another nearby home. Her heart beat a little harder to underscore the dark and light playing across his face. Those dark-blue eyes were narrowed and filled with desire—for her. Gulping, Emma nodded. They fell into step while avoiding the donkey-cart ruts down the center of the muddy street.

"So, how was your day?" Khalid inquired. Up ahead their transport helicopter sat like a dark hulk. As soon as the load master who guarded the helo returned from eating in the village, they would lift off and fly back to the base camp. No one kept a helo on the ground overnight out here.

"Busy," Emma admitted, smiling a little. "The women got all the school supplies divided among the children. They'll have everything they need for tomorrow's first class."

"Good. We got the desks all assembled, finished off some last-minute things in the room itself and now it stands ready for use." Khalid rubbed his hands and gave her a satisfied smile. "We've done good work today, Emma." And then he grimaced. Khalid hadn't meant to call her by her first name. That was personal, not professional. Giving her a quick glance, he saw her eyes widen considerably over the gaffe.

"I apologize for that slip," he murmured.

Emma couldn't be angry at him. The way her name whispered from his lips sent a tantalizing sensation across her skin. "I guess when we're alone, we could use first names," she said.

Holding up his hands, Khalid said, "I want what makes you comfortable. I know you prefer professional military conduct between us." Khalid didn't want that, but he had no choice. And it formed a buffer zone between them so that his aching need to kiss her, to court her, was stopped cold.

As she reacted to Khalid's earnest look, an old block in her heart melted. How long could she go on pretending she wasn't drawn to this heroic man? No matter what Emma tried to do, she could no longer erect Brody Parker's face and memory as a wall between her and this handsome pilot. "It's okay," Emma reassured him.

Relief and terror surged through Khalid. This was new footing, and it was like going down slopes with rocks that slid from beneath him. Instantly, he felt thrown into turmoil because the expression in Emma's eyes rocked his foundation. He saw desire in her eyes. For him.

As they approached the helo, the load master came out to meet them. Emma ordered him to the chieftain's house for dinner. His face lit up and he eagerly trotted back into the village. They climbed into the fuselage via the lowered ramp. Emma automatically swept her gaze around the bird to ensure all the cargo had been removed. The fuselage sounded hollowly as they walked toward the cockpit.

Emma took the right seat and sat down. Khalid hesitated a moment, pulled something out of his large right leg pocket and then sat down. Curious, Emma saw he had a small book in his hands. Looking out the window, she searched the area for movement as a matter of habit. The A-team had a member out on guard walking the perimeter around the helo. She knew the Taliban was active at this time of day. Like nocturnal animals, they stirred at dusk and hunted throughout the night.

For the first time, Emma spoke his first name. "Khalid, did you see those two boys? Those two poor little orphans who came in earlier today asking for help?"

Nodding, he placed the book on his thigh, his hand across it. "Yes, Benham and Fahran. Abbas took them in. With so many family members being killed by each side, children are left to fend for themselves."

"It's horrible," Emma muttered. "It just tears my heart out of my chest. Those two children had no shoes and they were wearing such thin clothes. I don't know how they survived the nights in these mountains."

"That was curious to me, too," Khalid murmured. "It's freezing at night. What they wore wouldn't keep them from dying of hypothermia."

"They probably slept in tight little balls against one another," Emma said. "They're so cute. Benham is shy. He wouldn't look anyone in the eyes."

"That's not uncommon. These children have PTSD and they're traumatized to the point that they don't know who to trust any more. They're orphans of war."

"Fahran told Abbas that they came here because they heard that Americans were giving food and clothing away."

"Word carries fast," Khalid said. He watched the soft gray dusk accentuate Emma's freckles. Once inside the helo, she'd removed the hijab and ruffled her fingers through her hair, catching the strands and taming them into a ponytail. Soft, curled tendrils along her temples emphasized the anguish in her green eyes. "Well," he said, "let me read to you from Rumi." He held up the book. "My father gifted me with this set of poems when I was five years old. You can see how dog-eared and worn the book is." He gave it a fond look as he lifted it toward her to inspect.

Emma could see that the title on the small red leather book was nearly worn off. She couldn't make it out. "Oh, so you're going to read to me?" Thrilled by the offer, Emma wondered why, but didn't want to spoil the magic of the moment. She was exhausted trying to ignore his masculinity, his worldliness and kindness toward others. Maybe, just this once, it would be all right, she told herself. All right to let down her walls and just be with him in this stolen moment.

"Of course," Khalid said. He opened the book and gently laid it across his thigh. The light of dusk filtered through the Plexiglas to highlight the words written in Pashto. "He is our greatest Persian poet and mystic. His words touch the soul of a person, regardless of their faith and beliefs. He was so connected to the Creator that he transcended his own Sufi boundaries to see that all of us are loved."

Sitting back in the seat, Emma watched Khalid's darkened form in the copilot's seat. She absorbed the grace of Khalid's long fingers. He reminded her more of an artist than a combat helo pilot. "I haven't had anyone do this for me except when I was a little girl. My parents would come in and read to me. I loved that time. I remember being in bed with my stuffed bear, Mr. Brownie. Mom would play the part of the woman in the story and Dad would be the man." Emma smiled in remembrance. "That was so much fun…."

"Reading is a way to open a person's heart," Khalid agreed. "It shows care, respect and love."

Emma felt her heart thud on that comment. Khalid's warm look stirred her body. He touched her on a level no man had ever reached. Emma was afraid to tell Khalid that, for fear that she would lose control. And that just couldn't happen.

"Well," Khalid murmured, "I have chosen some of my favorite quotes from Rumi that I'd like to read to you."

Just the way Khalid softly spoke the lines in his husky voice made her feel as if warm honey were being poured over her. Touched beyond words, Emma struggled to find her voice. "That was a beautiful poem." She considered Rumi's words for more than a minute. Khalid sat quietly, hands resting over the book balanced on his thigh. He seemed at peace, undisturbed by the war-torn world that surrounded them. "It sounds as though Rumi knew through experience about love."

Nodding, Khalid said, "Yes, Rumi knew the

great highs and lows of loving another just as we do. He had a great love and then it was torn from him." Khalid touched the edge of the book with reverence. "Rumi led a hard, demanding life. That is why I believe so many people around the world, regardless of their personal belief system, can relate to his poems."

Sighing, Emma looked through the Plexiglas at the graying world, "I've never known that secret sky he spoke about in his poem…." Then she caught herself, blushed and gave Khalid an apologetic look.

"There are many types of love," Khalid agreed. "Rumi, because he was a mystic and desired to know the Creator, walked through trials by fire in order to fulfill his desire. To do that, one has to experience these things as other people do. But—" Khalid smiled a little "—he knew love and many of his poems are a reflection of that. It isn't always love between a man or woman, it can be the love you have for your parents, your friends or your relatives."

"He sounds like he was a very astute observer of life," Emma said. "I really wish now that I had studied Rumi more back at language school. I like how he sees our messed-up world."

"Let me read you another poem," Khalid said, and carefully turned the page on the very old, well-used book.

Emma felt as if that poem was about her, about the walls she was trying to build within herself to stop herself from liking Khalid. Shifting uncomfortably, she refused to meet Khalid's inquiring gaze after he finished the reading. His expression softened.

"I know that something exists between us," Khalid began gently, getting Emma to look into his eyes. "I feel you pulling back, Emma. I think I understand why, or perhaps I don't at all."

Ouch. Emma sat up, hands clasped tensely in her lap. "Are you always this direct?"

"I speak from my heart," Khalid said. "I know no other way. Do you?"

The man was so open and vulnerable right now that Emma couldn't just fire off some sniping comment and escape from the helo. The sincerity in his darkened eyes called to her. "I…well…" she hesitated. And then, she knew she had to be equally honest with him. "Look, Khalid, you're my boss. I don't think a personal relationship is appropriate. Do you?"

"I wasn't expecting to be attracted to you, Emma." He never broke eye contact with her. "For so long, I felt nothing at all after Najela's death. In fact—" and he straightened and looked out at the darkening world beyond them "—I did not realize my heart was healing from that tragedy until I met you."

Emma sat immobile, confused. "Oh…" was all she could manage.

Khalid wrestled mightily with his past. After Najela's death, he'd sworn never to fall for another woman and put her into danger. Now his resolve was disappearing. All he wanted was a closer connection with Emma. The more he tried to stop himself, the more he felt driven to do the unthinkable.

Khalid could see the bewilderment on Emma's face. Without thinking, he stood and leaned over her. His hand slid across her jaw to cup her cheek. Bending his head, he gently placed his mouth across Emma's parted lips. Her breath was warm and sweet, her mouth soft and tasting of cinnamon chai. He felt Emma stiffen and then, surrender to his kiss. There was such hesitancy and, yet, a sense of yearning as her mouth slid provocatively against his. The moment felt torn out of time and place. All Khalid could do was taste Emma, absorb the perfume of her skin, her hair and the silk of her mouth into his wildly pounding heart.

Emma suddenly jerked out of the woven heat of the moment. She looked up into Khalid's hooded, dark eyes that burned with need—of her. "We can't!" she cried.

Khalid stepped back, hearing such fear in her voice. His mouth throbbed with the kiss, the taste of her on his lips. The book was still gripped in his hand. "I'm at fault," he murmured apologetically. "After Najela's murder, I swore I would never get involved with another woman. I never wanted her harmed as Najela had been." He gave Emma a helpless look. "I'm so sorry, Emma, I don't know what happened."

Emma felt panic. She could still feel the masculine stamp of Khalid's mouth on her own. Oh, how she wanted him! All of him! The unexpected kiss broke open the lies she'd been telling herself. His mouth resting lightly on her own, his male scent consuming her, all conspired against Emma. The raw pain in his hoarse tone was evident. Najela's death had changed him forever. Opening her hands in desperation she said, "We've both got good reasons not to do this. I'm relying on you to give me a positive rating after this mission."

Khalid shook his head, his emotions still gripping him in a powerful hold. "But I will give you an excellent report for your personnel jacket. Why are you so worried about that? You are a good pilot, you care and you're an excellent officer. How could I not give you a glowing report?" Khalid knew from many earlier heartbreaks that some women could not tolerate his Muslim-Christian background. Maybe that's what this was all about. He borrowed from both great religions, but primarily was guided by his Sufi heart and soul. His heart never led him wrong, but Khalid had encountered a few women in his life who were not as tolerant as he was, and those relationships had broken up as a result. Was Emma wrestling with this issue, too? It didn't matter. He had to be responsible.

Never would he place Emma in Najela's place. He just couldn't!

Khalid sat down. Emma looked as if she wanted to run away. Searching her face, he asked, "Is it because of my religions that I embrace, Emma? Does that offend you?"

Brows raising, Emma gasped, "Why—no! Of course not!"

"What then?"

Emma sighed. She had to tell Khalid why it was important to get a good grade on this mission. As quietly as she could, because she didn't want her voice drifting out beyond the helo to other ears, she confided in Khalid how she'd allowed Nike Alexander to give up her seat in the Apache to save a Special Force's sergeant's life last year. As she finished the story about the punishment she'd gotten, the demotion and the black eye it had given her famous military family, Khalid's expression changed from confusion to surprise and then, finally, understanding.

"Ah," he said, "I see why you are so distraught. It creates great pain for you to hurt your family's untarnished reputation. I get that." Khalid sat for several moments digesting Emma's conundrum. He could still taste her on his lips. He never wanted that sweet cinnamon taste to go away. The barrier between them was greater than he'd anticipated. And now he understood Emma's fear of intimacy with him.

"Can I convince you that I will give you a good mark for this mission?" he asked in a hopeful voice.

Emma grimaced. "So many things could go wrong, Khalid. It's not a matter of trust. It's about life. What if we got together and then broke up three months from now? You'd be hurt. Angry. And you could get even with me by giving me a very bad mark on the report."

Emma shook her head. "No, I can't risk that. I'm sorry."

Tapping his fingers softly on the book, Khalid said, "I wish I could regret kissing you. But I cannot." His stomach roiled, his heart pounded as if he were being pushed in several directions—between the horrific past, wanting to love Emma and knowing he never could.

Emma shrugged, dodging his inquiring gaze. She stared down at her clenched hands in her lap. She could feel Khalid struggling with these issues. Emma felt she owed him the truth. Looking up, she held his gaze. "No, I can't regret it, either, Khalid. But there are other things involved."

"Such as?"

"Such as I'm on a second tour over here. In nine months, it's finished and I'm being rotated stateside. I have three more years on my officer's contract with the U.S. Army. I have no idea where I'll be sent."

"I understand. Many hurdles."

"Yes," she whispered, feeling emotionally exhausted. "And they are all out of my control."

"But," Khalid persisted with a gentle smile, "life always throws hurdles at us. I swore on Najela's grave not to fall in love with another woman and have her harmed by Asad Malik."

Now more than ever, it was time to tell Khalid everything. He needed to know about her own heartbreak. She couldn't hold back. Emma finally broke down and told him about Brody Parker. When she was finished with the deeper explanation, she said unsteadily, "Just as you have your own reservations about getting involved again, I feel the best thing to do is to walk away. We can't jeopardize this mission… or our wounded hearts."

The words were like ice. Khalid realized he was just coming out of two years of grieving over the loss of Najela. He was acting irrationally and expecting too much from Emma. It was her right to set the agenda. "I understand," he said. "I will honor your needs, Emma. I will remember our kiss forever." Moving his shoulders, as if to remove an unseen load, Khalid added, "I do not want to be a dark shadow that stains your life and stops that wonderful smile from giving others sunlight."

Feeling miserable, Emma muttered, "I appreciate it, Khalid. I'm just sorry it couldn't be what we wanted."

Khalid rose because he saw the sergeant returning from the village. "I am, too. Here comes our load master. We need to fly back to base camp now."

"Hey," Nike Alexander called, sticking her head inside Emma's tent, "how are you?"

Emma was just easing her flight boots off her feet when her best friend slipped through the tent flaps. "Hey, Nike. Good to see you."

"Girlfriend," Nike murmured, putting her

hands on her hips and studying her, "you look like hell warmed over. Bad flight back from Zor Barawul?"

Sighing, Emma gestured to the chair next to her cot. "Have a seat," she said. After she kicked her boots beneath the cot, she got up and tied the tent flaps together. She'd just arrived back to Bravo an hour earlier. It was cold, nearly freezing outdoors. As soon as Emma had got in her tent, she'd turned on the space heater to warm it up.

Nike put her helmet bag next to the chair and sat down.

Emma poured herself some water. "Want some?"

"Yes, thanks. We forget we're in a desert, and none of us drinks enough to stay properly hydrated," Nike said.

Emma poured a second glass and handed it to the Greek pilot. "You look like you saw some action. There was a lot of chatter on the channel as I was flying back."

"Yeah," Nike said, drinking the water in gulps. "The crap hit the fan over near the border about three miles west of Do Bandi." Nike gave her an evil grin. "We creamed about fifty Taliban who thought they could sneak across the valley in the dark."

"Wow," Emma murmured, "that's good."

"Fifty that won't be harassing those poor Afghan villagers in that area," Nike said. She placed the emptied glass on a table next to where she sat.

"Yes, and Do Bandi is one of the villages we're working in to bring education to the children," Emma said, worried. She sat down on the cot next to her friend.

"So, what's with you? Catching the flu? Rough flight back? Get shot at?"

Mouth quirking, Emma growled, "I wish it was one of those things."

"Uh-oh," Nike said, grinning. "Man trouble."

"It's Khalid."

"Yeah, remarkable dude, isn't he? A stud. If I didn't love my guy like I do, I'd sure consider chasing him myself," she chuckled.

Emma searched her friend's face. "From the moment I saw him, I felt my heart twang like a harp. I fought it, Nike. I put up good reasons not to even think about being with this guy."

"But?"

"We were in the cockpit at dusk tonight. He came and sat down in the copilot's seat and started reading Rumi's love poems to me."

"How sweet!" Nike got excited. "Emma, that's wonderful! How many American guys would think of doing that?"

"Oh, you would react that way, Nike. Dammit! I need a little pity here, okay?"

Nike chuckled darkly. "What's standing in your way, Emma? You're not attached. And if you like him, what's the problem?"

Emma told her. She saw Nike lose some of her ebullience over the event.

"Oh yeah, I forgot about that. He is your boss, after all. And Brody Parker led you on and then crushed your heart. He was a sonofabitch."

"I really hurt Khalid's feelings tonight. He asked me if I trusted him to do the right thing. And I said I couldn't trust him."

Nike shook her head. "I feel for both of you. Right now, you're caught between a rock and hard place. Your first duty is to your family and expunging the bad name we managed to give it."

"Yeah," Emma sighed, "I know it. To be fair to him, he's fighting his attraction to me because he lost Najela to Asad Malik. He doesn't want to put another woman in that bastard's gun sights."

"Mmm," Nike said, "He's caught between a rock and hard place, too."

"Yes," Emma said, feeling glum.

"Well," Nike said, patting her friend's sagging shoulder, "you do the best you can, Emma. The way I look at it, if it's meant to work out, it will. No matter the reasons, if it's meant to be, it will happen. You have this mission to toe the line on and get glowing commendations."

Giving Nike a warm look, Emma gripped her hand, squeezed and released it. "I just want to try and get my career back on track and get my family's good name polished up again."

"Right on," Nike agreed.

Emma pressed her hand to her heart, her voice low with unshed tears. "The problem is I like the guy. More than a little. This sucks.

"Doesn't sound like a problem to me." Nike gave her an encouraging wink, which didn't help matters.

Chapter 9

"Brother," Kinah called to Khalid from the door of the school, "come visit with me."

Khalid halted in the center of the muddy street in Do Bandi. The late-April rains were starting once more. He wore his dark-green nylon jacket and a black baseball cap to shield himself. As he glanced over his shoulder, he saw that Emma remained at the CH-47, helping a group of medical people get their supplies. He hadn't seen Kinah in two weeks and he waved to her.

When Emma looked his way, Khalid motioned with his hand, signaling where he would be if she needed him. Today, he was the pilot and she was the copilot. It was her duty to deal with the details while he could be somewhat free from those responsibilities. Emma raised her hand in return and nodded.

Happiness thrummed through Khalid as he turned. A cluster of children surrounded him at the door where his younger sister stood. He pulled out handfuls of candy from the thigh pockets of his flight suit. Little hands opened. They didn't grab or fight. Instead, Khalid could see Kinah's firm but loving training.

"Well, well," Khalid said to them, "I believe you all need this." He handed out all the candy to the children. They were polite, smiling and they thanked him. Then, they scattered to the four winds, sweet treasures in hand.

Kinah laughed and stood aside so her brother could enter the now-empty classroom. "You are like Santa Claus to them, brother. And you spoil them. Every time you fly in here, they know it's you. I can hardly keep their attention when they hear your helicopter coming toward the village."

Khalid grinned, shut the door and embraced his tall sister. She was dressed in a cinnamon-colored wool robe and a bright-red hijab covered her black curls. "I can see your handiwork, sister," he whispered, giving her an evil grin as he stepped back. "They are acting with manners. Well done." Khalid scanned the area. "This looks great," he said. There were three large green chalkboards hung on three walls. Twenty-five desks were arranged in tidy rows. Kinah was one for insisting that children learn to be organized. Each desk had a notebook, a pen and a pencil on top of it.

Kinah slipped her arm around her brother's arm and walked him to her desk at the front of the room. "Do you have an apple for the teacher, too?"

"No," Khalid admitted, still smiling. "No apple."

Pouting, Kinah released his arm and sat down in her chair. She gestured for him to sit down in the sturdy wooden chair next to her desk. "I know, you save all your gifts for Emma."

Khalid sat down and took off his baseball cap. He shrugged and said, "Well, perhaps I did remember to bring you something." He dug into the pocket of his jacket. Kinah had a great love of Kit Kats, the chocolate wafer bars. She'd been able to get them only rarely after leaving America when her education was complete. He saw Kinah's winged brows rise, and she looked with curiosity at him.

"I met Steve Hudson, an army major at Bagram. He's assigned to fly with the Apache squadrons in the south. He just happens to be a good friend of mine. So I asked a favor of him…." Khalid drew out four Kit Kats and handed them to his sister.

Kinah gasped. "Khalid! You did it!" She grabbed them. "Oh, you are such a jewel, beloved brother!" Rapidly, Kinah tore off the wrapping and took her first bite of the Kit Kat.

Khalid laughed. "You look like an addict getting her fix, Kinah."

Giggling between bites, Kinah said, "Oh, I am! But better to be addicted to chocolate than opium."

On that note, Khalid lost his smile and became more serious. "Indeed," he murmured. It did his heart good to see his vibrant, feisty sister once more. Since Operation Book Worm had begun on April second, nearly four weeks ago, he'd rarely seen his sister. Kinah's job was to bring in teachers, create an atmosphere of learning and organize everything having to do with the children's education. Her tasks were at an end today at Do Bandi. Khalid and Emma would be flying her to Zor Barawul, where she would manage the educational program for two weeks, before they headed home today.

Kinah sighed, finishing off the first Kit Kat. "That was pure heaven. Thank you, brother." She reached over and pinched his cheek.

Khalid caught his sister's long, fluid hand and placed a kiss on the back of it. "You were looking tired. I knew Kit Kats would refuel you." He released her hand. Kinah colored fiercely and pretended to give him a stern look.

"Brother, I fly on the wings of my heart's passion. You know that. And when you love what you do, all the energy in the world is available to you."

"You have always been guided by your heart." She returned his look. "Is there any other way?"

"No," he agreed. Gesturing around the room he asked, "So, how are you? Have things been quiet here?"

Kinah sighed. "The last week has been peaceful. The Taliban, I think, realize that with an A-team stationed here, they cannot ransack and harm the villagers. It has been a very happy, relaxed place for once."

"Mmm," Khalid said. "The Taliban goes where there is no threat to them."

"That's getting hard for them to do with the border villages," Kinah said. "You should see the difference in the people here, Khalid. They are protected for the first time in many decades. They laugh. They smile. It truly warms my heart." She pressed her hand to her breast, tears in her eyes.

"The children look clean and their hair is cut and combed," Khalid agreed. "They are joyous. I can see it deep in their eyes."

Reaching out, she gripped Khalid's arm. "What we are doing, brother, is helping. I hope you know the extent of it."

"I do. But I always worry for you. Being out here alone…"

Kinah snorted. "I'm fine, Khalid! Do not look so anxious. Save your worry for that red-haired woman who stirs the fires of your heart." Kinah saw her brother suddenly lose all his vitality, his eyes dark. "What?" she demanded, leaning forward. "Khalid, what's wrong?"

"Oh," he murmured, "There is tension between Emma and me." Giving her an uncomfortable look, Khalid added, "We're drawn to one another, but neither can do anything about it for different reasons."

"What? The most handsome, richest man in all of Afghanistan? I know hundreds of young Afghan women who dream of you being their husband!"

Twisting in the seat, Khalid grimaced. "It's not that simple, Kinah. You know the military."

"Ohhh, my poor older brother! What could she possibly not like about you?"

Khalid held his sister's indignant look. "Emma likes me—"

"Well, there you go!" Kinah said, triumphant. "I was right! No woman worth her salt will not be swayed by your looks and kind heart."

"Kinah, let me finish…."

Pouting again, Kinah sat back in her chair. "Go on."

"Emma has a six-month mission assignment. Technically, I'm her boss as the military sees it. At the end of those six months, I must write a recommendation based upon her performance over that time."

"Emma is a hard worker!" Kinah said. "She's kind, responsible and cares. I'm sure you'll give her the praise she deserves in that report."

"Yes, I will." Khalid gave his sister a look, pleading with her to stop interrupting him. He told Kinah the rest of the story. When he finished, he added, "And so, she cannot get involved. If she did and we broke up, she's afraid

I would give her a bad grade and recommendation. That would hurt her military career. And
frankly, I hadn't thought of that angle at all. But
she's right."

Snorting again, Kinah leaped out of the chair
and began to pace the room. "This is silly stuff,
Khalid. I see how Emma looks at you. I certainly see the look on your face. Clearly, you
are both falling in love with one another!" She
threw up her hands and looked at the ceiling.
"Surely, Allah, you can get these two stubborn donkeys together? Rip off their individual
blinders so they can see?"

Khalid chuckled over his sister's dramatic
antics. "Kinah, come, sit down...."

"How can I, brother? Surely," she protested,
turning and standing in front of him, hands on
her hips, "this is really about trust."

"Yes, it is," Khalid said, looking up at her demanding features.

"Emma doesn't trust you."

"That's right. She says I'm like the man who broke her heart. He too was rich and powerful. Only, he was married with two children, and he lied to her."

"Of all things!" Kinah stamped her foot and then said, "I will talk to her. I will tell her how sweet, how kind and how sensitive you are. That you would never break someone else's trust."

"No," Khalid said, "you can't talk to her, Kinah. It wouldn't be right. I'm hesitant to get into a relationship, too." He frowned and his voice lowered with anguish. "I can't because I want no woman murdered and tortured as Najela was. As long as Asad Malik lives, I will put no other woman beneath his sword. You know that. I've purposely avoided getting back into a relationship for two years now because of that price."

Rolling her eyes, Kinah muttered, "Men! You're all alike. I swear by Allah, you are!" She cupped his jaw and looked into his anguished blue eyes. "This must stop, Khalid. You can't put your life on hold because Malik is a threat. We may never see him die, and what will you do then? Live life as a monk? Deny yourself the happiness you deserve?" Removing her hand she straightened. "Khalid, do not be afraid to live once again. Don't be scared of reaching out to Emma if she stirs your heart. Asad Malik wins if you deny yourself any sort of personal life." She marched to the door and pulled it open.

Alarmed, Khalid leaped to his feet. "Kinah! Where are you going?"

"To see your beloved," she sang out, sailing out the door and disappearing.

Khalid groaned, knowing he couldn't make a spectacle of himself by rocketing out of the room and running down the street after Kinah. What had he done? It would only make things worse if he intercepted Kinah in front of Emma. And his sister wasn't one to be stopped from her trajectory. Khalid knew she cared for him and she liked Emma. It was Kinah's way of caring: getting involved as a possible future sister-in-law. Frustrated, he stood looking at the light filtering into the classroom. Emma wouldn't be happy about this. And his sister had a goal in mind, Kinah was mission-oriented. Groaning again, Khalid decided the best thing he could do was visit the chieftain of the village, give his regards and find out if he needed anything from the U.N. forces.

"Emma!" Kinah called, waving at her. Emma stood near the ramp after giving the medical team directions into the village.

"Hey, Kinah!" Emma's smile blossomed genuinely for the firebrand woman. "How are you?"

"I'm fine, my sister." Kinah gave her an American hug and then the Afghan greeting of kissing her cheeks. Gripping Emma's upper arms, she said, "Are you feeling well?"

Emma laughed. "Yes. Why? Do I have dark circles under my eyes?"

Kinah took her hand and pulled her away from the A-team members who were walking the perimeter of the helicopter. "Come with me," she whispered dramatically. "We must talk."

Emma warmed to the small Afghan woman. The bright-red hijab reminded her of a red light flashing on a police cruiser. Smiling to herself, Emma allowed Kinah to pull her aside. The rainy skies threatened. A shaft of sunlight shot through like a beam down into the green valley far below. The wind was chilly and Emma was glad to have on her thick nylon jacket.

"Now," Kinah said, releasing her hand and remaining near Emma, "it appears to me that your heart has dark circles beneath its eyes!"

Studying Kinah's narrowing gaze, Emma

said, "What?" Sometimes Kinah spoke in symbols and she couldn't follow the intelligent woman at all. Plus, Kinah, who loved all things American, mixed and matched Afghan sayings with American slang and sometimes, it all got jumbled for Emma.

"Do you like my brother?"

Before Emma could speak, Kinah held up her index finger the way a teacher would to a child.

"Before you say anything, my sister, I want to know how you feel. Not what you think." Smiling brightly, Kinah pressed her hand to her heart. "And no, Khalid did not send me out here to harass you. I've decided to find out the truth for myself."

Unable to stop her smile, Emma quickly grasped what was happening. Sometimes, Kinah's excitement and sureness sent her like a juggernaut into a situation or in this case, into a person—her. "Did Khalid tell you why I can't like him?"

"Oh, pooh!" and Kinah waved her hand impatiently and wrinkled her fine, thin nose. "Whys do not count, sister. Only your heart counts!"

Emma rested her hands on her hips and appreciated Kinah's misguided efforts. "I'm sure he told you why I can't cross that line."

Widening her large eyes, Kinah whispered fiercely, "Yes, he told me. Emma, why do you deny your heart its yearning? My brother likes you. Allah knows, he moons like a dog that has lost its mate. He told me why you think you cannot like him, but I say this is foolishness. How often do you think love happens between two people? Not often. And you deserve happiness, Emma. I know my brother will make you ecstatically happy."

Emma held up her hands. "Whoa, Kinah. Slow down, okay?"

Laughing, Kinah shook her head. "Slow down? Does the heart ever slow down? Of course not. Emma, I know you care very much for my brother. When you think I do not see the look you give him, or that he gives you, I remember it." Kinah tapped her temple. "You are suited to one another. Perfectly. I see no reason not to allow Khalid to court you as is our custom."

Emma saw the burning hope in Kinah's eyes. She was incredibly beautiful, with a square face, a stubborn chin, gorgeous high cheekbones and a broad brow. Emma had wondered many times why Kinah had never married. Surely, she'd had suitors. Emma made a mental note to ask Khalid sometime about that. "I love you dearly, Kinah, but there can't be any courting. I'm sorry, but my life belongs to the U.S. Army. I'm not as free to follow my heart as you think." She touched Kinah's proud shoulder. "I think the world of Khalid. You're right: he's an incredible man and truly deserves happiness after losing Najela. But I'm not in a position to do anything about it, Kinah."

Touching Emma's reddened cheek, Kinah whispered, "You are wrong, but I understand better what Khalid had told me about the two of you. I see that there are other priorities that must be sorted out first."

Emma smiled gently. She loved Kinah's fierce independence, her willfulness, her heart brimming over with a desire to lift others and give them a better way of life. "That's a nice way of putting it," she told her.

"And what if these priorities sort out?" Kinah asked, slyness in her tone.

Emma chuckled. "Oh, you're such a crafty fox, Kinah! Just be patient. I don't know what the next minute will bring. Or the next hour. In our world of the military, all I can count on is change."

"But you like my brother?"

"I do," Emma hesitantly said.

"Does he not melt your heart?"

Sighing, Emma nodded. "He can melt butter with those looks he gives me sometimes."

Clapping her hand, Kinah said, "Wonderful! I have prayed to Allah daily that my dearest brother would be healed of his wound and loss. I prayed that a new woman might enter his life, awaken his numbed and shocked heart." She gripped Emma's arm, giving it a small shake. "My brother is one of the finest men you will ever meet. He appears kind and gentle, but he carries the heart of an Afghan snow leopard. He is a warrior, but he knows when and how to display that side to himself. He can be your best friend, Emma, if you allow him that. Perhaps that is all you can share with one another right now, but allow him that at least."

"You're such a used-car salesman, Kinah."

Kinah laughed. "Thank you, dear sister. That is a compliment! Afghans are great traders, as you know."

When the Silk Road existed, Emma knew,

Afghanistan was little more than four hundred different tribes. And they traded lapis lazuli, the bright-blue stone, for much money and goods. Trading was, indeed, in their DNA. "Yes, *you* certainly are." She looked at her watch. "Kinah, I have some things I have to attend to."

"Of course," Kinah said. "I'll meet you here once I find my handsome brother."

Emma watched the elegant Kinah turn and walk with pride in her steps. Unable to be angry over her overture, Emma hurried up the ramp to find the lists that she had to check. She wondered if Khalid knew that his sister had come to plead his case with her. Somehow, Emma felt Khalid would be embarrassed by it, but who could stop Kinah?

Chapter 10

Back at base camp, Emma walked with Khalid over to Ops. There they had to fill out the mandatory after-action flight reports. The April skies had cleared and now a cool breeze blew across the area. Helicopters of all types were coming in before night fell. Only the Apaches with their 24/7 ops ability ruled the night air.

Khalid opened the door for her and they made their way to a small room off to the left of the busy Ops desk. After shutting the door, Emma set her helmet bag on an empty table, grabbed the report forms and sat down. Khalid did the same.

"So," Khalid said as he looked up from his form, "my sister grilled you. I'm sorry, Emma, I didn't want her to say anything."

Touched by his sincere apology and the worried look in his blue eyes, Emma stopped herself from reaching across the table to touch his hand. How easy it was to let herself simply be lulled into Khalid's world of the heart. "Don't worry about it." Emma pushed some strands of hair off her brow. "Kinah is a force of nature that no one can stop. She was very nice about selling you to me."

Khalid sat back and looked up at the ceiling for a moment. "I knew she'd do that…."

"Hey," Emma murmured, sympathetic. "She loves you, Khalid. She's a great sister. I have sisters, too, and I'd want them to circle the wagons to support me."

"Do they?" he asked, resuming work on his report.

"Yes. We're tighter than fleas on a dog."

Laughing at the slang expression, Khalid shook his head. "Well, I ask your forgiveness for my beloved but impetuous younger sister."

"I weathered it," Emma said dryly.

After filing their reports, Khalid prepared to check out an Apache helo. He would fly it back to Bagram Air Force Base. Emma rose and collected her gear and walked to the door. Outside the thin wooden door she could hear the noise of Operations: the laughter, the people talking, along with the sound of airplane and helo engines.

"I'll see you tomorrow at 0800?" Khalid asked as he opened the door. How badly he wanted to romance Emma, but he knew it was folly. If anything, Khalid realized his growing desire for Emma would truly have to be tabled forever. The pain in his heart was constant over that realization.

"Yes," she called over her shoulder. Emma lifted her hand in farewell. "Have a safe flight home, Khalid."

He watched Emma disappear in the crowded Ops and his heart contracted with sadness. Turning, he walked up to the Ops desk to fill out a flight plan before he left for Bagram.

Emma was jolted out of her early-morning sleep by a sergeant who came to her tent.

"Captain Cantrell?" the woman sergeant called.

Disoriented for a moment, Emma said, "What? What's wrong?"

"Ma'am, Zor Barawul is under attack. We need every available pilot!"

Adrenaline shot through her and she leaped off the cot. "Has Captain Shaheen—"

"Yes, ma'am. He's on his way to pick you up

right now. You have about ten minutes before he arrives here at the base."

Emma turned on a small lamp that gave her enough light to get dressed and hot foot it over to Ops. "What's the report on the village? Do we have Apaches in there?" Grabbing her flight boots, she jammed them on her feet.

"Yes, ma'am. Two Apaches were sent there about thirty minutes ago when the attack by the Taliban began."

Emma quickly caught her red hair into a rubber band at the nape of her neck. She stood up, grabbed her helmet bag and rushed out the tent flap. The sergeant trotted alongside Emma. Overhead, the night sky twinkled with bright, white stars. A thin slice of moon hung in the sky. The air was cold but not freezing.

"What else?" Emma demanded, jogging down the road between lines of tents.

"Ma'am, they think it's Asad Malik attacking.

It's his signature and the A-team is calling for reinforcements."

"Dammit," Emma muttered. Her brow wrinkled. One of the things they had done after they left the village of Do Bandi was to take Kinah north to Zor Barawul. She was to spend the next two weeks helping to get the teachers set up to teach. Was Kinah okay? Emma's heart contracted with fear for the woman.

The sergeant said, "Ma'am, I need to get back to BJS HQ."

"Fine, I'll be in radio contact with HQ on this, too." Emma lengthened her stride, fully awake now. By the time she arrived at Ops and signed in, she saw Khalid's Apache landing outside the doors. Once outside, Emma stood impatiently on the tarmac and waited until the blades had stopped turning. The flight crew quickly placed chocks beneath the three wheels.

As she quickly climbed up on the helo, she saw Khalid's dark and tense face. The other cockpit behind his had the canopy open. She hesitated for a moment. "Khalid, have you heard anything on the attack?"

"No, climb in."

Nodding, Emma swung into the seat and quickly got settled. A crew woman helped her strap in and then closed and locked the canopy before hopping down off the helo and pulling the ladder away. Time was of the essence. As soon as Emma got the helmet on her head and plugged into the communications system, she asked, "What's the last you heard, Khalid?"

"Let's do the preflight check. I'll tell you more after we get airborne," he ordered tersely.

The tension in his voice heightened Emma's worry for Kinah. Oh, God, what if she was hurt? Emma's hands flew with a knowing ease as she went down the check list for preflight with Khalid. Her heart pounded like a drum and speed was important.

The Apache shook and shuddered around

them as Khalid, the air commander, got the helo up to speed. Emma received permission from the control tower to take off. She noticed that the Apache was loaded with weapons. They were flying into combat, no doubt.

As the helo took off beneath Khalid's hands, Emma switched to the green light across her instrument panel and two screens in front of her. The green color was less harsh on her vision. Blackness surrounded them, the base camp quickly disappearing. They would fly at nine thousand feet toward Zor Barawul. Emma felt safe within the shuddering vibration of the Apache. She could sense Khalid's worry. What must it be like for him? He'd already lost the woman he loved. Now, he could lose his sister. Emma knew how close they were, how much they loved one another. "How are you doing?" she asked.

"The best I can," he growled.

Emma heard the terror in his low, husky tone.

She could hear his fast and shallow breathing. "Does Kinah know what to do in a situation like this?"

"My sister is a survivor, if nothing else."

"And she's gone through attacks like this before?"

"Yes."

His voice was raw and strained. How would she feel if one of her sisters was in a fire fight with the Taliban? If the Taliban broke through, they'd kill Kinah on the spot. Lips tightening, Emma said in a soothing voice, "I know she'll be okay, Khalid. I feel it in my heart."

"Let us hope you're right," he rasped.

There was little else she could do. Emma felt a special kind of helplessness. She knew all the people at this village. Good, kind and generous Afghans who wanted nothing more than a life better than the hard-scrabble one they had to eke out in these desert mountains. And what of the A-team stationed there? Had they taken

casualties? Emma couldn't stand not knowing
so she dialed in the A-team frequency. Instantly,
her ears were filled with the sound of gunfire,
explosions and the yelling of orders between the
captain and his men. No doubt, a fierce, ongoing battle. Gulping, Emma began to pray because at this point, that's all she could do.

Khalid circled the village of Zor Barawul,
high up on a hill far above a narrow unseen
valley below. His heart centered on Kinah, but
he couldn't afford to go there. Right now, he
was coordinating with the two Apaches already
on station and working to kill the Taliban who
had gotten very close to the village itself. In his
gut, Khalid knew it was Asad Malik. Just the
other day on a Taliban website, he'd read that
Malik promised to kill him and Kinah. Was this
the beginning of his campaign against them?
Khalid had read Malik's spewed hatred against
the education of girls. He'd railed against Kinah

because she was a woman leading a fierce battle for peace and education.

Khalid had not told Emma about this website or Malik's promise. Grimly, he swung the Apache around as the air commander, Major Klein, ordered them to hover and fire rockets into a hillside about two hundred feet below the village. Unable to do anything but focus on the attack, Khalid worked constantly with Emma, who would handle the ordinance and fire the weapons.

Emma watched the explosions walk across the rock, dirt and thick scrub brush on the steep slopes. She heard Major Klein ordering another set of Apaches out of this fire fight, saying that they were low on ammunition. They would have to fly back to the base camp, take on another load of ordinance and then fly back here. Emma was amazed at the ferocity of the battle. The winking red and yellow lights of A-team members firing down the hill looked like Christmas sparkling in the night.

Emma worried for all the villagers, like Ateefa, the little girl with the prosthetic leg. How was her mother, Jameela? Was she holding her children and trying to keep all of them safe? In the mud homes, bullets could easily fly through the walls and kill someone trying to hide. Abbas had one of the few stone houses, but it had windows and bullets took no prisoners.

Her headphones jumped with more frantic calls from the A-team. A group of Taliban had breached the slope! She felt Khalid moving the Apache in that direction. With a sinking feeling, Emma saw the other two Apaches who had been on station flying off because they were out of ammunition. Now, it was up to them. Could they repel this attack? Hundreds of infrared bodies showed up on the slope via the one screen. The Taliban were like relentless ants crawling up the hill and cresting it.

"Medevac's on the way," Emma reported, hearing another channel. "A-team has four men wounded."

"Roger," Khalid growled. "Switch to Gatling gun. Hose that area where the enemy is getting over the top of that hill."

"You got it," Emma said. She felt the Apache bank, heard the engines thunder as her fingers flew over the console to engage the huge gun beneath the belly of their helo. At least twenty Taliban were now running full tilt toward where the A-team had made their stand. If they got past the A-team, they were into the village itself. And Emma knew they'd go house-to-house, firing inside and killing everyone without mercy. The villagers had some weapons but could never repulse an attack like this. They were helpless against these thugs.

Khalid took a big risk by flying in low. They

were well within range of the enemy firing a grenade up at them, or worse, a rocket. It was a chance they had to take. The helo shuddered violently as Emma triggered the Gatling gun. Khalid felt the floor of the helo vibrate heavily as the gun continued to fire. His feet grew numb from the shudder. He watched his other cameras because he knew Emma was engaged with the gun.

Suddenly, a bright light popped off the slope about two hundred feet below. "Rocket launch!" he yelled. Instantly, he shoved the throttles to the firewall, hit the rudders and made an effort to evade the fired rocket.

Emma cursed and quickly turned her attention to it. She hit the flares in the nose. They could possibly detour the rocket. Red flares lit up the sky. Her fingers flew to the trigger to fire their own rockets. She punched the button. Instantly, the Apache bucked from the rocket's fire. Bright yellow light momentarily blinded her. Her harness cut deeply into her shoulders as Khalid worked frantically to get the Apache out of the way of the oncoming Taliban rocket. Her eyes widened and her heart banged violently in her throat. Would the rocket hit them?

A million thoughts jammed into Emma's head as she watched, almost fascinated, as the ground-fired weapon hurtled up toward them. A rocket had heat-seeking abilities and she was sure it had locked on the Apache's overhead engines. Mouth dry, Emma suddenly felt her entire world slow down to single frames from a movie. She heard Khalid's heavy breathing. Felt the Apache screaming in protest as he continued violent, evasive maneuvers to try and outwit the oncoming rocket.

Then, at the last second, the Apache rocket locked onto the enemy fire and struck it with full force. The entire night lit up like a Fourth of July celebration. Emma gasped and threw up her gloved hand to protect her eyes from the red, yellow and orange fireball that was no more than three hundred feet to their starboard. The resulting explosion sent a massive shock wave through the night air. It struck the Apache broadside. The helo shuddered and shook. Khalid wrestled with the controls in order to ride out the shock wave.

"Direct hit!" Emma yelled, her adrenaline pumping through her, making her anxious and yet angry. She had no time to sit and gloat over the fact they were still in the air.

"Back to work," Khalid snarled. "Gatling gun. We're going back in. The Taliban is still on top of the hill. We've got to stop them!"

For the next ten minutes, Emma's world revolved around halting the Taliban attack. Her headphones crackled with other communications. There were three medevac helos on the way. Khalid asked BJS 60 to send more reinforcements, saying that they were running low on ordinance. Emma was careful with the

Gatling gun. Prolonged firing would only waste the precious ammunition. Instead, with Khalid's expert touch at the controls, she was able to use the infrared camera that showed body heat and fire it in short bursts. It saved their ammo and targeted the running groups who were trying to penetrate the village itself.

Sweat poured down Emma. Her gloves were wet, and she felt the trickle from beneath her armpits. Her gaze was glued to the television console, slipping back and forth between it and the infrared screen. Emma saw the Taliban being driven to a standstill. In the back of her mind, she worried that another rocket would be fired at them. They hovered less than four hundred feet above the fray and directly over the A-team like a big, bad guard dog. Bullets pinged off the Apache's resilient skin. The Taliban were now firing up at them, hoping to hit the rotor assembly above the cockpits and bring them down.

Time became suspended. All Emma saw was gunfire back and forth. The shuddering of the Apache vibrated through every cell in her tense body. Khalid's breathing was ragged and so was hers. This was a life-and-death effort. If they couldn't stop the Taliban from coming over the slope, the A-team would be overrun. Already, the A-team leader had called for reinforcements. They needed more ammunition. A CH-47 had been launched from the base camp with a resupply of ordinance for them, but none of it would get here in time. Emma knew it was only their being on station above the team that might tip the balance in their favor. If they hadn't hovered and stood like a gate guardian, the Taliban would have surged like a tsunami into the village, murdering men, women and children.

"Fire a Hellfire missile into that area where they've breached it," Khalid ordered her.

Emma rasped, "Roger that…" She quickly

dialed in the Hellfire II. It was a brilliant idea. Why hadn't she thought of it?

"After firing it, I'm going to fly us around to attack that slope with what we have left in ordinance. If we can't stop them, everyone's toast."

"Roger," Emma said sharply, her mind focused on the missile. She flipped the switch. The Apache jerked as the missile slid off the rail. Light flared beneath the stubby wing. And then, she watched it hunt down the mass of men coming over that slope like a dark, malevolent ooze toward the village.

The entire night sky lit up again. Blinded, Emma couldn't know how many that rocket had killed, but it had to be substantial. Rock, dirt and dust flew skyward. She felt Khalid wrenching the Apache in a sharp bank to the left. The shoulder harness bit hard into her and Emma tried to brace herself. Khalid was a skilled pilot and he knew how to push the limits of the Apache to get the maximum performance.

The helicopter thumped down, down, down the slope where there was no longer any enemy left alive. Emma tensed and held on. She worked to get the gun back online. In seconds, Khalid whipped the combat helicopter around to the slope where the Taliban had breached the hill. On the screens in front of her, Emma observed a lot of unmoving bodies. Down below them, however, was another mass trying to climb upward.

"Fire at will," Khalid muttered.

"Roger," Emma said, her voice taut. She triggered the gun again and again. The knot of Taliban scattered like a flock of birds that had had a rock thrown in their midst. "They're on the run!" she yelled triumphantly.

"Keep at it," Khalid ordered in a tight voice.

Between her skill at hitting targets and Khalid's ability to make the Apache dance like a ballerina in the sky, Emma was able to beat back the rest of the attack. In minutes, the charge was over. They swung around and around the hill looking at their infrared screens for any moving bodies trying to form another attack. Sweat ran into her eyes. Emma blinked several times. She pushed the perspiration away with her trembling, gloved fingers. She felt the Apache surge upward into the darkness.

"I think we got them," she told Khalid. Her voice was shaky; the adrenaline made it that way.

"Roger that," Khalid agreed, his voice thick with unspoken emotion.

"We're down to dregs on ordinance," she warned him.

"In five minutes, two more Apaches will arrive on scene."

Five minutes could be a hell of an eternity, but Emma remained silent. They kept flying around the thickly brushed slope below the village. Who was dead in Zor Barawul? Who was injured? She could hear the chatter between the

A-team leader and the medevacs that would arrive on scene in ten minutes. Before they could land to take on the injured men, the place had to be secured and safe. That was their job: fly around and continue to be a threat to the Taliban, should they think of trying a second assault.

"Helluva night," Emma whispered into the microphone on the inter-cabin frequency.

"Yes. You're a good shot."

She heard a little relief in Khalid's voice. He was on an adrenaline high like her. Emma smiled a little. "You're one hell of a pilot, too."

"Thank you. Now we're a mutual admiration society."

Chuckling, Emma felt some of her own relief tunneling through her. "I'm worried about Kinah. I wish we could know how she is."

"I know…"

"Maybe we can get one of the A-team to go check in the village as soon as medevac arrives and takes their wounded back to the hospital at Bagram?"

"That's what I was thinking," Khalid said. He swung the Apache out in wider arcs as they approached the base of the hill where the village sat. "I wish we could land. But I know we can't."

Emma grimaced. "Take it from one who once did and suffered as a result, you don't want to do that."

Khalid smiled, but grimly. He kept his hands on the collective and cyclic, continuing to widen their hunt for whatever was left of Malik's group. He hoped Malik was dead. "No, I don't want to go there. When things get organized and calmed down, we can ask the captain to send a team member in to locate Kinah."

Emma saw the other two Apaches arriving on station. It felt good to see the combat helicopters loaded down with ordinance. "Whew, the cavalry has just arrived. Good to see them."

"Hey, Red Dog One," Nike Alexander called to them, "I hear you've been stomping the hell outta the Taliban. Good work. Doesn't look like there's anything for us to do. Bummer! Over."

Chuckling, Emma keyed her mike. "Roger Red Dog Three, we didn't leave much for you to clean up. Over."

"And here I wanted to dance on those bastards' heads," Nike chortled. "Over."

Khalid laughed and so did Emma. "We're going to hang around for a while longer, Red Dog Three. Over."

"Roger that. More Apaches are good. It will give those bastards second and third thoughts about regrouping to hit this village again. Any idea of casualties yet? Over."

"No, Red Dog Three. No sense of how many are dead or wounded. Over."

Emma sat back and tried to relax as Khalid urged the Apache to five thousand feet. She watched as the other two combat helos scoured the area, hunting like hungry wolves for any survivors. Grateful to this incredible machine, Emma knew they had saved Zor Barawul. At least this time. She wondered how Khalid was handling the fact his sister might be dead or injured. How badly she wanted to land, but they didn't dare break that regulation.

Emma switched to inter-cabin and asked Khalid, "You doing all right?"

"As best as I can. I'm worried for Kinah...."

"What if we get permission to fly back to camp and then we pick up a CH-47 and fly back out here? It will be dawn by that time and we'll be able to do it. That way, we can land and you can find Kinah. It might take an hour, but at least you'd be on the ground." A CH-47 had no nighttime gear on board and was only flown in VFR conditions where the pilot could do a line-of-sight visually.

"Good idea, thank you."

"I'll call BJS and get permission to head back to base," Emma said.

Chapter 11

"Kinah!" Khalid called as he ran into the village shortly after Emma had landed the CH-47. Dawn crawled up the horizon, allowing them to fly back to the battered village. The A-team leader, Captain Jason Cunningham, had radioed in just as they landed the Apache at their base camp. They'd found Khalid's sister. Kinah had been wounded in the fierce fighting but had waived her right to be brought back on the medevac. There were men on Cunningham's team that needed medical treatment before her own wounds, she'd told them.

As he rushed into the schoolhouse, Khalid saw that hundreds of bullets had punctured the mud walls.

Kinah sat holding the two orphan boys in the schoolroom. "Khalid!" she cried, relief in her tone.

"Sister!" he rasped, his voice cracking with emotion. Kinah's hair was in disarray. Small oil lanterns burned and shed light into the gray space. Beneath each arm huddled one of the young orphans, Benham and Fahran. Both were pale, their eyes huge with fear. She sat on the floor, her back to one wall near the desk. She was not wearing a hijab. Tracks of tears streaked down her dirtied, tense face, making Khalid even more anxious.

"They said you were wounded," he whispered, kneeling down and tentatively touching her shoulder. He tried to keep the fear out of his voice as he searched for blood.

"Just a scrape," Kinah protested, sniffing. She held up her hand and showed him a graze of a bullet across her wrist area that had been hidden by her robe. As Khalid gently cupped her shoulders, she struggled to battle back her tears. Her lower lip trembled. "Khalid, it was awful! So many people were killed! I hate the Taliban! They did this to us!" More tears fell and made tracks through the fine dust across her face.

"I know, I know," Khalid soothed. He crouched before them. Gently touching each boy's head, he asked them in Pashto if they were all right. Each jerkily nodded they were okay. Khalid could see they were in shock by the glassy look in their eyes.

"I was in here," Kinah whispered, "with them. They wanted to help me clean up the room. Such good boys." She wiped her eyes and sniffed. "It was just shortly after dusk." Looking around at the holes and the cool air flowing through the schoolroom, Kinah sobbed once and then gulped back the rest of her tears.

"I dragged the boys beneath my desk and huddled with them in my arms. We were all crying, Khalid. We were so afraid. I've been in fire fights before, but this one was the worst I've ever weathered. I was fearful of the Taliban overrunning the A-team. Poor Captain Cunningham! He and his men fought fiercely. All I wanted to do was keep the boys safe and survive this awful hell on earth!"

Touching her curly, dusty hair, Khalid gave her a sad smile. He pulled a green linen handkerchief from his pocket and gently dabbed her dusty cheeks. "It was bad," he agreed. "But you survived, Allah be praised. And so did these boys." He gave them a smile in hopes of letting them know they were now safe. "Are they wounded?"

"N-no," Kinah sniffed. She took the handkerchief and wiped her eyes. "A medic already came by and checked them over. He wanted me to leave for this silly scratch on my wrist and I told him no. The boys are fine. Just scared."

Who wasn't? Khalid nodded and helped each boy to stand. They shook like leaves in the wind. He then gripped his sister's hands and pulled her to her feet. Khalid briefly held her, placed a kiss on Kinah's damp cheek and looked deeply into her frightened eyes. His sister had been in two other villages where fire fights had broken out a year ago. This one, however, had scared her even more and shadows lurked in her brown eyes. "I want you to come home for a while, Kinah. Let the U.S. Army get this place more secured. Then come back here."

"No," she muttered, giving him a defiant look. Breaking free of his embrace, Kinah brought the two boys to her side and held them. Each clung to her robe.

Sighing, Khalid nodded. "I thought you'd say that."

"We can't leave. That would be a sign of defeat, Khalid. You know that." Kinah scanned the room riddled with bullet holes. "No, I refuse to run! I would say this is the work of Malik." Her brows dipped and anger tinged her husky tone. "That desert rat is behind this, Khalid. My gut tells me so. Last year up north at the other village where I worked so hard to get the people to build a schoolroom, he came in and shot hundreds of holes through it."

"Yes," Khalid said quietly, "I believe he's behind this attack." And he said no more. Both of them were aware of Malik's promise to kill them. It had almost happened last night. Khalid wanted desperately to remove Kinah from the village. As he looked into the stubborn set of her chin, he knew it was useless to insist.

"Where's Emma?" Kinah asked, wanting to move on.

"At the helo. We brought in a medical team and other emergency supplies." He glanced toward the door that had been splintered by gunfire. "I need to get back to help her. Will you be all right here?"

"I'm fine, brother. Go. I'm taking these boys to my home. They need to get washed up, find clean clothes and be fed some food. That's where I'll be."

Khalid leaned over and pressed a kiss to her damp cheek. "We will come to see you later," he promised, his voice thick with emotion. Turning on his heel, Khalid left the nearly destroyed classroom. A number of the desks were in shattered ruins, too. His heart ached for his sister. This time around, Kinah had been brutally impacted by the attack. The other two times last year were nothing in comparison to this one. Khalid could see that she grappled with the trauma of it all. Who didn't in this demoralized village?

* * *

Emma glanced up to see Khalid striding down the muddy street toward where she stood with the list of supplies in hand. How was Kinah? Anxious, she passed the list to her load master. A number of men from the village assisted what was left of the A-team to offload the emergency supplies. Five soldiers were on their way to Bagram for treatment of their wounds. The medical team, consisting of a doctor, a nurse and a medic, was already in the village helping those who had been hurt, but not badly enough to be medevaced to Bagram for treatment.

Meeting Khalid, she asked, "Kinah? How is she?"

Khalid told her. The morning was dawning clear after the storm clouds of yesterday. Emma's fine, thin brows moved downward as he finished.

"She's been traumatized," Emma growled, unhappy.

"Yes, this time it really got to her," Khalid agreed, his voice distraught.

"She won't leave?"

"No. Wild horses wouldn't drag her out of here now."

Seeing Khalid's worried, forlorn eyes, Emma wanted to reach out and embrace him. "I'm sorry, Khalid. War is ugly business. Everyone is hurt by it," she said, hurting for him.

"You should have seen those two orphan boys. They were shaking like little trees in the aftermath."

"The worst is how the children are affected," Emma agreed. "But they're with Kinah. She'll be a rock for them and she'll get them through this."

Khalid looked around. Bodies of the Taliban had been put to one side of the flat landing area. A number of Afghan national soldiers had come with them on their flight, and now they were

going through each man's clothing to find iden-
tification. It wasn't a job he would want.

"Malik's behind this," he rasped to Emma as
they walked back to the helo. Most of the crates
were out of the bird and the last of the A-team
men hefted supplies on their shoulders and took
them into the busy village.

"It sounds like his signature calling card: destroying the schoolroom. The bastard," Emma
whispered, angry.

Walking up the ramp, the load master, a
twenty-year-old blond technical sergeant
handed her another list. Emma stopped and
signed it. She was AC, air commander, and
therefore responsible to see the shipment was
out of the helo and delivered to the proper village authorities. Khalid walked past her and
sat in the left-hand seat. He moved his knees
aside so she could slide between the seats and
sit down in the right-hand seat. Even though

she was the AC, Khalid was the head of this mission.

"What now?" Emma asked. Khalid's profile was silhouetted against the sunlight suddenly flooding into the cockpit.

"I need to talk with Abbas. By the way, their family is okay. Shaken up, but no injuries. Many of their windows are shattered, but they can be replaced."

"Good," Emma sighed. "I'm relieved." Living in a stone house rather than a mud one had its advantages in a fire fight.

Khalid glanced around. No one was near their helicopter. Driven by the anguish of his sister facing death so bravely, he couldn't help himself. Last night as he and Emma had fought the Taliban, he'd known that they, too, could die. And they nearly had when that rocket was fired at them.

Khalid's eyes narrowed upon her, burning with desire. Taken off guard by his sudden predatory look, she didn't see it coming. One moment he was in the chair and the next, he was standing. He cupped her face with his long hands and leaned down, sweeping a powerful kiss against her mouth. Emma stiffened momentarily. The heat of his mouth rocked her lips open. She felt his warm breath, smelled his spicy scent and tasted chai.

Her world dissolved beneath the swift, hungry kiss, his mouth sliding hotly against hers. Oh! Emma didn't know what to do. For so long, she had yearned for Khalid's mouth on hers once more. She wanted to feel his sensuous, exploring lips against hers, inciting her, teasing her and letting her know just how much he loved her.

Mind spinning as she hungrily returned his passionate kiss, his fingers moving through her hair and holding her prisoner against his searching mouth, Emma heard the word *love* reverberating through the halls of her wildly beating heart. Right now, Khalid's mouth was playing her as if she were a beloved instrument in his hands. His lips drifted from her mouth to her cheek, to her closed eyes and finally, back to her parted, wet lips. There was such tenderness in Khalid's slow exploration of her as a woman. And Emma wanted this. She wanted him.

Khalid's soul absorbed Emma. Never had he wanted a woman more than her. That shook his internal world. His grief was gone. In its place an assuredness that this magnificent and courageous red-haired American woman was priceless to him. Her mouth was soft and pliant, giving and taking. He'd been afraid she'd reject him, but, to his relief, once his mouth slid across hers in invitation, she'd responded just as eagerly and passionately as he. Perhaps it was the combat last night, their near-death experience? Khalid wasn't sure. What he did know without reservation was that he was falling in love with Emma.

As he sipped at her wet lips, Khalid smiled and whispered against them, "You are the sunlight to my darkness, beloved."

Just the way he whispered *beloved,* made Emma moan with pleasure. As she drew away, his face inches from her, the tender light burning in his blue eyes, she didn't know what to do or say. "Oh, Khalid," she managed in a strangled tone.

"I know," he said apologetically, releasing her. "We're in a very confusing situation." He stared down at her full mouth glistening in the wake of his worshipful kisses. Fighting himself, Khalid sat down. He reached out and gripped her hand. "We could have died in combat last night."

Emma closed her eyes, as she heard the urgency in his voice. She worried about someone seeing them kiss or holding hands. It was forbidden by military law. Opening her eyes, she cast a quick glance around. They were alone, and relief sped through her. She drowned in his pleading gaze. "In our business," she said in an unsteady tone, "we can die at any time, Khalid. You know that." He had been right, though. Last night's combat had been raw and violent. She was still edgy from it. So was he. Plus, Khalid had thought his sister might have died in the attack. Emma realized the pressures upon him and knew that he needed a safe harbor. She was that harbor.

Nodding, Khalid forced himself to release Emma's hand. It was a hand he wanted to kiss, one finger at a time. His dreams were erotic, with his loving Emma an inch at a time. "Yes, you're right. I'm still on an adrenaline high from it."

Emma tucked her hands in her lap. "We're both jumpy. We have a right to be." She lowered her voice and searched his stormy gaze. "You could have lost Kinah last night. I understand, Khalid. We all need someone at times like this."

The silence settled in the cockpit. Khalid's

heart pounded with love for Emma. He knew he could not speak of it. Not yet, at least. And he had to get past the six-month mission before he broached it with her. "People need people," he agreed, his voice suddenly weary. "I'm just glad you're here. Thank you." He reached out and grazed her hand. "I didn't exactly give you warning, did I?"

Emma drowned in the heat of his voice and eyes. Khalid's ability to seduce her was more than impressive. She'd never met a man who could touch her heart and soul at the same time. But Khalid did. "No, you didn't," she admitted, her voice barely above a whisper. What should she do? As much as she tried to push away her desire for Khalid, their attraction kept growing. Emma felt out of control, but reasoned that it had to do with the combat.

"It was good."

His eyes crinkled at the corners. Sometimes, Khalid reminded her of an Irish elf, a trickster who was completely unexpected in his actions. Like this kiss. How long had she waited for it? Emma wanted to tell Khalid of her dreams of making love with him, but she didn't dare. "Yes, it was very good," she said. "But I'm confused, Khalid. I'm not sure what to do."

"Then," Khalid said, hope in his voice, "perhaps we can learn to be good friends who support one another in times like this?"

"I don't know where professionalism and personal needs begin and end with you. I'm at odds with myself." She touched the area of her heart. "I wish we'd met somewhere else. The military is a rough place to find romance, much less keep it and grow it."

Joy raced through Khalid as he heard Emma's softly spoken admittance. She couldn't look at him, her gaze down on her tightly clasped hands. He wanted to unleash his excitement and hope, but he reined it all in. He had to respect Emma's need to get past this mission. "You have trusted me with yourself, Emma. I will hold you in my heart and hands as if you were a dear friend."

Tilting her head, Emma studied Khalid's serious features. "I've been in other situations where my boss and I did become friends. It never influenced us when we were flying or what we had to do in our respective jobs."

"And you are okay with that between us? To allow our friendship to flourish like a red rose bud?" Khalid asked hopefully.

She melted beneath his burning blue eyes that spoke so fervently of untold and unexplored possibilities. Perhaps, someday, Emma cautioned herself. "I can't think of having a better friend than you, Khalid."

Chapter 12

"You're looking pretty down," Nike observed of Emma as they sat in the chow hall at dinner time. The place was noisy, crowded and plenty of A-teams were mingling with the combat and transport pilots.

Emma pushed the mashed potatoes around on her aluminum tray. "Yeah, some stuff happened in the last twenty-four hours, and I'm conflicted about it."

Nike had her appetite. She dove into the steaming mashed potatoes and gravy. "Khalid?" she guessed.

Looking up, Emma frowned. "Yeah. How'd you know?"

Nike wiped her mouth with a paper napkin. "Oh, come on! He's in love with you. Don't you see it?"

"Mmm…."

Nike cut into her sirloin hamburger. "The guy clearly loves you. Now, I wouldn't ordinarily judge things like that, but it's written all over his face every time I see him with you. Has he let you in on his secret?" She grinned wolfishly.

Unhappy, Emma set her cutlery aside and sighed. "Yes and no. He kissed me this morning." Emma saw Nike's black, thin brows raise with surprise and then she saw fear in her friend's eyes—for her. Holding up her hand, Emma quickly added, "No one saw us."

"That's good. Because you think getting busted over us landing on that hilltop was something? If Dallas hears about you kissing another officer in a combat zone, your ass is grass, my friend. You'll never be more than a captain, even if you're allowed to stay in for your twenty years."

"I know, I know."

"So, you want his attention? He seems like such a heroic figure, Emma. He's doing so much for his people here in his country. He and his sister are out on the front lines every day making a difference." Nike popped some food into her mouth, chewed for a few moments and swallowed. "What's not to like?"

"I didn't want his attention, Nike, but he's a man with a mission."

"You like him?"

"Yes." Emma's brows curved downward and she stared at the food on her tray, her stomach in knots. "There's nothing to dislike about Khalid. That's the problem."

Nike studied her critically. An entire A-team took up the picnic tables to their left. She lowered her tone and leaned forward so only Emma could hear her. "What is the problem? That he's Afghan and you're an American citizen? That your family, if they heard about you falling in love with a foreigner, would go bonkers? Or...? You supply the third reason."

Emma glanced toward the A-team. A sergeant came and sat to her right, his tray filled high with food. She knew these men ate MREs out on their thirty-day missions and that hot food was a rarity in their lives. "My family is very open-minded about whom I might fall in love with. My mom and dad aren't prejudiced."

"Yeah," Nike said, "but he's a Muslim, Emma. Did you consider that angle? I mean, the Trayherns are a military dynasty. I'm sure you probably don't have that religion in your family."

Emma shrugged. "Not yet. My family accepts all religions, Nike. They have a live-and-let-live attitude. I like my parents' take on it: a religion is something you live daily. It's not about going to church once every seven days and then not living your beliefs the other six days. In Khalid's case, I respect and admire him for his dedication and beliefs. He clearly lives them every day whether it's dangerous to do so or not. That's commitment."

Nike considered her words. "I just wonder if your parents would be so open-minded if you married the guy, though."

Shocked, Emma sat up. "Married?!" She'd said it a little louder than she'd thought. The entire A-team to their right collectively lifted their heads and stared at Emma. They soon turned, bent their heads and continued to shovel in the food as if they'd never get any more.

Heat flushed from Emma's neck upward and stung her cheeks. She rolled her eyes, having no one to blame but herself for speaking too loudly. Nike grinned, clearly enjoying her reaction. Emma leaned forward and whispered, "I haven't thought of marriage, Nike."

"Well, I didn't either when I met Gavin, but that's what happened," Nike chuckled, resuming eating her meal.

"Did your family have issues with him being an American army captain because you're from Greece? Did your parents get upset with the fact you are going to marry someone who wasn't Greek?"

Nike wiped her mouth, took a sip of her coffee and said, "No, they didn't. My dad was in the military for twenty years and is now a commercial pilot for a major Greek airline. He flies around the world. My mother is cosmopolitan, too. The only thing that gives them stress is that when I marry Gavin at the end of our tours, we'll continue to be in the army. And so, we're not going to be home in Greece. They'd like that, of course, but understand we have to go where the army assigns us."

"Yes, but eventually, you will retire," Emma said. "Would you live in Greece or the U.S.?"

"We don't know that yet. My parents want us to live in Athens near them. But Gavin's farm parents want him to come and settle down near them in Nebraska. We're not promising either set of parents anything at this point."

"And Gavin isn't Muslim," Emma muttered.

"True, but you know what? I have a lot of friends who worship different gods. As long as they don't push their religion on me and I don't push my beliefs on them, we're fine. Everyone has to be more open-minded."

"It's only the fanatics of any religion who cause trouble," Emma agreed.

"So, if Khalid's religion isn't really an issue with your parents or you, why are you so hesitant?"

Emma picked up her fork and ate a few kernels of corn from her tray. "I just need time, Nike. I didn't expect to like this man. I didn't realize how heroic he really was deep down. Khalid has worked for the good of the common

people here in his country ever since he returned from the U.S. And it's not like he doesn't
have money. His father is a billionaire times ten.
He uses the money to lift people out of the terrible poverty we see here."

"Yeah, he'll need billions to do that," Nike
muttered. "With all the bribes that are expected,
I'm sure he goes through plenty of dough."

Emma groaned. "Yes, bribery has been a
way of life for Afghan people for thousands
of years. It's awful. I don't see what or who is
going to break this cycle, Nike. The chieftain
of the region is always looking for money from
Khalid."

"Oh, you mean Jawid Khan. He's a crafty
devil," Nike agreed with a slight smile. "But
he's like all chieftains. They have over four
hundred and fifty different tribes that make up
the country of Afghanistan. They've had this
system enforced for thousands of years."

Emma continued to nibble at the corn. "Khan

is only forty-five years old and, really, he's the one who is part of the Northern Alliance that has been fighting the Taliban for the last decade after the Russians gave up and left."

"I heard he's a pretty colorful guy. I've never met him."

"I haven't, either," Emma said, "but Khalid knows him well. He can't do business in Khan's villages without his blessing."

"And of course," Nike said, smiling, "the blessing is in the form of money greasing the chieftain's palm."

"Right on," Emma said.

"But, I hear from Mike, Dallas's husband who works up the strategy with the general, that Khan is a pretty decent fellow. He's continued to use his five hundred horsemen to seek and root out Taliban all along the border."

Emma nodded. "Khan is a good guy of a sort. I just wish this bribery would go away."

"But how else is Khan going to feed his men,

take care of his horses and get ammo to fight the Taliban?"

"I know, I know," Emma muttered. "It's a system. I don't have to like it."

"It's so old that I don't care what the commanders say about winning the hearts and minds of Afghans. I don't think it's ever going away," Nike admitted.

"I understand from Mike that Khan is coming to Zor Barawul. After this last attack on Khan's main village, he's shifting his forces to protecting them in a proactive manner."

"He's going up against his old nemesis, Malik," Nike said.

"Yep, those two hate one another. I'm hoping that with five hundred horse soldiers in the valley, Malik will think twice about doing what he just did to that village."

"Malik's not dumb. He's a cagey fox," Nike agreed. "He'll probably shift his force north or south of Zor Barawul."

"Yeah," Nike said unhappily, "to Do Bandi,

another of Khan's villages he's sworn to protect."

"At least we know the players," Nike said, lifting the cup to her lips and sipping. After she set the white mug down on the table, she added, "And Khan is a pretty good guy. Maybe Zor Barawul will get the peace it needs in order to really establish that school for the girls and boys."

Emma lifted her fingers and crossed them. "I hope so."

"You going out there tomorrow?"

"Yes, with Khalid. Kinah's in the village and we're bringing in a dental team for the children."

"You'll probably meet the colorful Khan, then. He's supposed to be arriving there by tomorrow morning, from what I understand."

Emma at his side, Khalid stood by the ramp of the CH-47 as Chieftain Jawid Khan, astride his prancing white Arabian stallion, rode up. In his hands, he had a box of dates from Saudi Arabia, one of Khan's favorite delicacies. The forty-five-year-old chieftain was tall and erect in the saddle. He wore a dark-green robe embossed with gold threads. The geometric designs across his powerful chest and sleeves emphasized his authority. On his head was a turban that matched his intelligent forest-colored eyes. Khan's beard was trimmed and neat but showed silver among the black hair. Khalid smiled to himself. Khan was from a thousand-year-old family line that had ruled this part of Afghanistan. The man was married and had ten children. The last twenty years of his life, he'd lived on horseback and fought, first, the Russians with the Mujahadeen, and for the last ten years, the Taliban, whom he hated with equal ferocity.

The stallion snorted and danced to a stop. It was decked out in a dark-green leather bridle and martingale, with gold tassels sparkling in the morning sun. The entire village of Zor Barawul had come out to welcome their leader and his five hundred horsemen now surrounding the entire mud and stone village.

Khan's narrow face broke into a smile. He'd lost one of his front teeth many years ago to a bullet that had grazed his mouth as he'd charged up a valley to destroy a Taliban machine-gun position. The bullet had chipped the tooth, but that hadn't stopped him from continuing the charge up the hill. When the fight was over and won, Jawid Khan celebrated with his men. He'd had his second-in-command, Naraiman, pull what was left of the tooth without any anesthesia. Out here there were no painkillers. Khan's men had roared and cheered as Naraiman used a pair of rusty old pliers to get the job done. Khan knew men would only follow a leader who didn't show weakness to pain or suffering.

Dismounting with a flourish after two of his

soldiers ran up to hold the stallion's reins, Khan grinned widely. He opened his arms toward the lean pilot in the dark-green flight suit. "Khalid, my brother!"

Khalid bowed his head to the mighty warlord and handed him the box of dates. "My Lord Khan. Welcome."

Khan looked at the dates and grinned. He handed them to another awaiting soldier. "Brother, you look well." He moved forward, kissed each of Khalid's cheeks and then shook his hand. Then, he turned and studied Emma whose red hair flashed like fire in the morning sunlight. She wore a hijab to match the color of her hair. "So, who is this beautiful red flower?"

Emma held out her hand to the warlord. She murmured the usual words of welcome and expected him to shake her hand. Instead, after giving her the formal greeting, Khan swept forward and kissed each of her cheeks, denoting that he considered her a trusted friend, not just an ally.

Breathless, Emma felt the soft brush of his beard against her cheeks. The man was very good-looking, despite the gap in the front of his upper teeth. His skin was darkly tanned, the squint lines at the corner of his green eyes deep and fanned out. Khalid had warned her that Khan was a flirt with all women, whenever he could get around Muslim law. In his position of power and authority, he regularly broke Muslim customs.

"So, Captain Cantrell, you are more beautiful than the stories that are carried to me." Khan stepped back and grinned up at the tall Afghan pilot. "Khalid, you are a blessed man."

"I think so," Khalid said with a slight bow of his head. "Come, we have gifts for you, my lord." He led Khan to the rear of the helo. "We have five hundred pounds of grain for your horses. We've brought in a pallet of five-gallon plastic jugs of water." Khalid knew that in this desert, food and water were scarce for man and animal. It was a worthy gift for the warlord, who appeared properly impressed.

"Very good, Khalid!"

"And," Khalid said, walking up inside the helo and bringing out a gunny sack that he held gingerly, "a special gift for you."

"Eh?" Khan's thick black brows rose as he took the gunny sack. Bottles clinked inside. "Is this what I think it is, brother?"

"It is," Khalid said, smiling. Khan had gone to school in France. He had a degree in Business Administration. While there, Khan had acquired a taste for good burgundy. Oh, Khalid knew that Muslim law forbade the drinking of alcoholic beverages, but that had never stopped Khan. "There are six bottles of burgundy in there, my lord. I think you will enjoy tasting them. A little reminder of France."

Khan grinned. He had sent his family to live

in France. He left them every spring and re-turned to them as winter set into his country. No one fought on horseback during the season of ice and snow. In France, his family was out of harm's way. In the winter, Khan ran several multimillion-dollar businesses in France that kept his family accustomed to their rich life. "Thank you, brother. You make my heart smile." Khan handed over the gunny sack to another soldier. He gave him orders to take it to the stone house which was always maintained for his visits to Zor Barawul.

Turning, Khan rubbed his hands together. "So, let us sit, have hot chai, breakfast and discuss things." He turned and gestured toward Emma. "Come, sister. You will join us as we talk strategy against my brother, Malik."

Emma was shocked by the invitation. Khalid had warned her that the westernized Khan paid no attention to the Muslim law that said men and women should not eat together. She saw

Khalid barely tip his head forward. "I'd be delighted," she told the warlord in Pashto.

"Excellent! Come!" He slid an arm through one of each of theirs and led them through the village. The villagers lined the rutted, dusty street. They cheered their proud warlord, for without him, they would have been destroyed by the Taliban long ago. If not for Khan's threatening presence, his five hundred loyal men on horseback, this village would have been utterly destroyed long ago. They had reason to cheer for their brave and caring warlord.

"And so, Malik attacked with at least two hundred men last night?" Khan asked, popping a date into his mouth. His men hovered nearby. The room had been prepared with expensive Persian carpets and many pillows and the scents of chai, curry and honey filled the air.

Khalid sat in the position of honor to the right of the warlord. Emma sat on the left. "Yes, my lord. And they almost overran us. Our three Apache helicopters made the difference."

"I wish I'd been here!" Khan said. He smiled over at Emma. "I understand you fly this Apache?"

"I do, my lord."

"Isn't that amazing, Khalid? A woman flying a combat helicopter."

Khalid understood Khan's amazement. In his country women were kept back from such achievement, something he wanted to change one village at a time by educating the women. Once they were educated, they could take places of more power, and their voices would be respected by the elders. "As you know, women in the Americas and Europe are not held under a man's thumb."

Grinning, Khan took a cup of chai from an old, bald man who was his chef. "Yes. One day, brother, I hope to see our women in those powerful machines."

Emma gulped and hid her surprise. Was Khan that forward-thinking? She stole a look over at Khalid, who seemed pleased. She knew these two men had at least a fifteen-year relationship with one another.

"I believe we will see our women rise to whatever they dream of becoming," Khalid murmured tactfully. "I hope in another decade, our country can be at peace, not at war."

Frowning, Khan sipped his chai. "So, tell me of Malik. Give me the details."

Khalid told him everything. When he was done, he added, "If you are going to stay in this area, it will be helpful. My sister, Kinah, refuses to leave this village until all is in order. We have teachers coming in to teach and they must feel safe here. Otherwise, they will leave."

"Of course, of course." Khan handed the emptied china cup to his cook. "But you know I have many villages to protect. I cannot remain here forever."

Khalid nodded. "How long can you stay?"

Pulling thoughtfully at his beard, Khan said, "Perhaps a month, brother. But I will need your help. I intend to root out Malik from the caves on the other side of this valley. I will not sit idle. And to do that, I need ammunition, food for my men, water and grain for my horses. We will hunt by day and return back here to Zor Barawul at dark."

"Whatever you need," Khalid promised, "you will have." Ammunition for their AK-47s and older rifles was vital. "And we have an A-team who will ride with you. They can call in bombs from B-52s and other aircraft should you flush out Malik and his men."

Khan rubbed his hands together in glee. "Excellent! We had another A-team ride with us for a month up north and they did a good job of calling in the bombs on the Taliban."

"Captain Cantrell and I will fly back to the base camp," Khalid said. "We'll let General

Chapman know what your needs are. It may take three or four days to get in all your supplies...."

"That is fine. My men could use a few days of rest," Khan said before smiling over at Emma. "We will rest. I will pay my respects to Abbas and the other elders. I will find out Malik's tactics from them. And then, when you return with our supplies, we can make our plans."

Getting up, Khalid said, "We'll leave now, my lord. Thank you for your generosity and food."

Emma quickly rose, bowed and murmured parting words to the smiling warlord. Outside the rock house, Emma walked at Khalid's side. The everyday rhythm of the village was once again in place. The children were playing, dogs were barking, women in burkas were hurrying down the street. Several carts drawn by small gray donkeys moved along the main thoroughfare. "Wow, Khan is something else!" Emma exclaimed.

"Yes, he's quite a colorful character," Khalid said, smiling. Down at the end of the street sat their emptied CH-47. The load master waited near the ramp. "Khan liked you."

Emma snorted. "I respect him for what he's done to try and keep his people in his villages safe."

"I meant," Khalid amended, grinning, "he was very drawn to you. I think he was enamored with your red hair."

Groaning, Emma muttered, "Great."

Khalid chuckled. "Don't worry. He knows that I favor you."

Feeling heat tunneling into her cheeks, Emma gave him a dark look. "We're friends, remember? Not an item."

Holding up his long, expressive hands, Khalid laughed as they stepped out of the village and onto the landing zone where their CH-47 sat. "Yes, yes, of course." Emma's worried look dissolved. Khalid was falling in love with this red-haired woman, with her dancing green eyes. For her sake, though, he had to slow down. She was obviously tense about the possibility of their relationship going beyond a friendship. He'd given much thought to Najela's murder and now was awakening from his loss. Kinah's words had shaken him. She had been right: he couldn't continue to live in a vacuum and ignore his need for a deep, satisfying relationship. Still, Khalid was nagged by Malik's presence and worried for Emma.

As Khalid entered the helicopter, Emma on his heels, he cautioned himself to remain patient. He had. Yet, he wanted to kiss her again. This time, he would trail a series of kisses from her silky, flame-colored hair all the way down every inch of her body to her toes. Khalid did his best to tuck all his longing away and sat down in the left seat as the copilot. Today, Emma was the AC of this mission. As he slipped into his harness and Emma sat down in the right-hand seat, Khalid wondered privately if she was falling in love with him. Was there hope for them despite this war?

Chapter 13

The early-June weather was welcome to Emma. She pulled off her helmet as Khalid squeezed between the seats and walked toward the opening ramp of the CH-47. The sunlight was bright and she was glad to have her aviator glasses on. Getting up, she set her helmet in the copilot's seat and smiled to herself.

Ever since Jawid Khan had made his presence known in the southern part of his territory, the warlord seemed to have chased Malik and his men out of the area. Despite Khan's presence,

Emma didn't trust Malik. He had twenty years of hard-earned camouflage techniques and could dig in, hide and still be nearby without anyone knowing about it. On the other hand, Khan knew how to dig rats out of a tunnel and he and his men had systematically scoured every cave along the other side of the valley, ridding themselves of pockets of Taliban. Khan took no prisoners and Emma saw the fierce horsemen in a completely new light. They were ancient warriors come to life. There was no mercy between enemies. Ever.

Today, MREs—Meals Ready to Eat—oats for the horses and more burgundy for Khan had been flown into Zor Barawul. Pulling the rubber band off her ponytail, Emma allowed her shoulder-length hair to flow free for a moment. She then combed her fingers through the strands and whipped her hair up into another ponytail. She grabbed her green silk scarf and wrapped it around her head. Once it was secured, she set off to visit with Kinah and see how things were going with the school.

There was an air of celebration in the village. A number of children who had been let out of school early were with Kinah, waiting anxiously at the edge of the landing area. The dust had cleared. Khalid worked with the A-team Special Forces soldiers and the load master to remove the supplies from the bird. About fifty of Khan's horsemen sat just out of range of where their helo had landed, their faces alight with expectation. They didn't necessarily like the MREs, but it was food. Many times, the horsemen had only meager supplies to last days at a time when out hunting the Taliban. Some days, they had nothing to eat.

Kinah waved and grinned. She refused to wear the burka that the other women of the village donned when outside their house but she wore the hijab. Her bright red scarf emphasized her black hair and flashing eyes.

"Emma!"

Emma grinned. "Hey, Kinah! How's it going?" The knot of children remained around her friend. She spotted the two orphans, Fahran and Benham, among the group. Ever since the horrific attacks by Malik a month earlier, the two had seemed inseparable. Kinah had saved their lives and they doted upon her.

Emma handed out candy to the children. Little hands shyly reached out, along with murmurs of thank you. She loved that these children were always polite and didn't grab a handful of candy and then run off. They knew how to share.

"I'm fine, sister." Kinah embraced Emma and they shared cheek kisses with one another. "Look at you! How long has it been? Two weeks? And Khalid looks very happy, too." She gave Emma a sly look. "So, love flourishes, eh?"

Emma stepped back and smiled. "We are just *friends,*" she emphasized.

"Mmm, friends. Indeed." Kinah smiled and looked across the sun-splashed narrow valley at the caves that were a part of the rocky landscape. "Friendship is always a good beginning basis for a relationship."

"It can only be friendship," Emma said. She fell in step with Kinah, the children providing a phalanx around them as they walked into the village.

"As you say, my sister," Kinah murmured, a sly smile still lingering across her mouth.

Emma wasn't taking the bait. She knew Kinah wanted her to fall in love with Khalid and marry him. Emma waved as a number of women in burkas came outside their mud homes to greet them. The village had a palpably, happy atmosphere. It was amazing how the people rebounded once the Taliban threat had been removed. Apaches had flown in almost daily during the first two weeks when Khan had begun to root out Malik and his men from the valley caves. The Americans had worked in concert with the warlord to eradicate the threat.

Kinah stopped at the school, opened the door and stepped inside. Emma followed and so did the curious children. Closing the door, Emma saw that all the bullet holes had been patched over with new mud. The temperature was pleasant, in the seventies and the windows in the schoolroom provided good light.

Emma scanned the room and looked approvingly at Kinah. "This is a wonderful space. It's as good as new. How are the kids doing?"

"They are learning to read and write not only in Pashto, but in English. I have told them that English is the accepted universal language for our globe. They must learn it in order to grow."

Emma nodded, glancing toward the books, the chalk, the crayons and at the children's art that adorned the walls. "Good. That's a wise move. Little kids are sponges and it's the right time to teach them foreign languages."

Kinah counted heads and then gave the children an unexpected recess, much to their delight. They would get fifteen minutes to go out and play. The classroom fell into silence as the last child left and closed the door. Kinah sat down at her desk and gestured to Emma to take a seat on the wooden chair next to it.

"My brother looks very happy, my sister. Have you two been growing closer as friends?"

Emma cleared her throat and sat down. "Yes and no. The military doesn't foster much else between officers other than follow the Code of Conduct. Fraternization is not allowed."

"Yes, that is what Khalid said."

The door opened. It was Benham, the thirteen-year-old orphan.

"Mem sahib, come quickly!" he called urgently. "There is a baby goat stuck in a thick bush down on the side of the hill. We need your help in order to free it."

Kinah frowned. "But, Benham, where is

the boy who tends those goats? It is his job to free it."

"No, no, mem sahib. This baby is far down the hill. Fahran and I can hear it bleating. It is in trouble! Can you help us? Please?" He gave her a pleading look.

With a sigh, Kinah got up. "Very well. I'm such a sucker for babies who get tangled up in all that brush."

"I'll go with you," Emma said, rising. She pointed to her flight uniform. "I can probably thread those thickets a lot more easily than you can in your robe."

Grateful for the company, Kinah nodded. They followed Benham out the door. He led them down behind the classroom. Emma saw nothing but a lot of thick green bushes. Some were two or three feet high and others, six to ten feet high. She saw holes in the ground where brush had been blown away by Apache rockets earlier. The wind was breezy as they stood on

the lip of the hill. It was a steep, rocky descent.
Benham scrambled like a mountain goat in his
new leather shoes down the reddish slope.

"Come, come!" he hollered enthusiastically,
waving them to follow him.

Emma heard a faint bleat. It was way down
the hill. She wore a .45 strapped over her Kevlar
vest across her chest, and she swept the area
critically for enemy. Yes, Malik and his men
had just been cleared, but Emma sensed the
enemy was never very far away. Malik was a
coyote. Looking over at Kinah, she saw the
woman scowling.

"Over here!" Benham called pleadingly, as he
slipped and slid farther down the rocky slope.
"You don't want the baby goat to die, do you?
I'll need help!" He slipped in between two thick
bushes and disappeared. The goat bleated again.

"Let me do this," Emma said, holding out her
hand as she took a step down onto the narrow,
sliding earth and rock. "You stay up here,

Kinah. You'll just get in trouble with that robe you're wearing."

"Are you sure, sister? This isn't the first time I've helped untangle a baby goat or sheep from that awful brush."

Grinning, Emma slid farther down the slope, arms out for balance. "My turn."

"Be careful..."

"Don't worry," Emma muttered, sliding and correcting constantly, "I will be."

Kinah noticed the other orphan, Fahran, suddenly appear out of the brush. He was farther down from where Benham had disappeared. His face was white and he seemed frightened. Kinah waved to him and called, "Emma is coming to help you. Just stay with the baby. She'll be there in a moment."

Fahran looked back toward the brush. He clung to a branch in order not to fall farther down on the steep talus slope. He opened his mouth and then shut it. Then, he looked at

Emma who slid down the slope toward him. Dust rose in her wake. Rocks tumbled all around where she placed her flight boots. More than once, Emma fell on her butt, got up, dusted herself off and kept moving toward where Benham had disappeared earlier.

"It's all right," Kinah called reassuringly to Fahran. The ten-year-old orphan had a soft spot for all babies, animal or human, she had discovered. Maybe because he had lost his own family, he was sensitive to the plight of others. Fahran clung to her gaze as if she were going to cast him off some day, but Kinah always reassured him that she would be there for him. "Emma is coming! Just stay where you are, Fahran!"

Emma disappeared into the brush. The shrubs were long-armed, poking at her, and the leaves swatted her face. Breathing hard, she watched where she put her feet. She could barely see anything, the brush was so thick. The goat bleated frantically now, but she couldn't see him, only hear him.

"Benham?" she called.

"I'm here, I'm here," the boy's voice drifted toward her.

"Keep talking so I can find you!" Emma called, holding up her arm to protect her face from thick foliage.

"You're coming the right way," Benham shouted. "Hurry, hurry! The baby goat is bleeding! You must rescue him!"

Groaning, Emma threw caution to the wind and crashed forward through the brush. She heard the baby goat. It was shrill and bleating, as if completely frightened out of its wits. "Damn goats," she muttered.

Just as Emma turned around to avoid a huge group of limbs and allow her body to create an opening, a man's hand grabbed at her shoulder.

Emma was jerked hard into the brush. Grunting and terrified, she looked up to see an Afghan soldier grinning at her. His fist was cocked, and it smashed down into her face. The moment his fist connected with her cheek, Emma felt an explosion of pain. And then, darkness.

"Khalid! Khalid!" Kinah screamed as she ran down the street toward the helicopter.

Khalid jerked around. His sister was white-faced, her eyes wide with fear, her hands above her head to get his attention.

As he handed the load master the supply list, Khalid stepped off the ramp. What was wrong?

Kinah raced to him, out of breath. "Khalid, something terrible has just happened!" She rapidly told him the story.

Frowning, Khalid knew that slope was precarious and steep. "Are you sure?"

"Yes, yes," Kinah sobbed worriedly, "I kept calling for Emma. She never replied!"

"What about the boys?" he demanded, feeling sudden fear.

"They're gone, Khalid!" Kinah pressed her hands to her mouth, tears streaming from her eyes. "Oh, brother, I think Emma has either been killed or taken prisoner by the Taliban! Otherwise, she would have returned my calls and the boys would have reappeared."

A cold terror bolted through Khalid. There was no way to get a horse down that slope. He ordered Khan's soldiers to get off their animals and follow him. As he raced down the center of the village, his throat ached with fear—fear for Emma. Khalid jerked his pistol out of the holster.

Kinah watched from the top of the hill as Khalid and fifty of Khan's men searched every inch of that slope over the next half hour. She had directed them to where she last saw Emma, and they had literally torn the shrubbery apart looking for her.

After a frantic search across the slope, Khalid scrambled back up the hill. He was breathing hard, his face a mask of fear. "I'm going to call this in to our base," he told Kinah. "Emma is gone."

"Oh, no…" Kinah moaned. She grabbed Khalid's arm. "I'm so sorry, so sorry. I should have known it was a trick. This is Malik's work. He's used the two orphans to lure Emma into their trap. Oh, Khalid, why didn't I see it? Why didn't I recognize this was a trap? What will they do to Emma?" Her eyes were wide with terror.

Khalid gulped hard and pulled loose from his sister's grip. "I've got to go. I'll get back to you as soon as I can. Use the radio I left with you if Khan's men find anything or if you hear any-thing from a Taliban envoy."

Kinah gulped and rasped, "Yes, yes, I will, my brother. This is terrible! Emma's in danger!"

She was in more than that and Khalid knew

it as he raced down the dusty road toward the helicopter. His mind spun with what had to be done first, second and third. His heart was pounding in agony. *Oh, Allah! Emma is a prisoner of the Taliban!* He knew it in his gut and heart. Najela's dead body swam in front of his eyes. Running up the ramp, Khalid snapped orders to the load master to get the supplies out of the helo pronto. Fifteen men from the village raced forward to follow him.

With a steady voice, Khalid talked to BJS 60 ops, telling them everything. A CH-47 did not have infrared or television cameras. He couldn't just lift off and fly around to try and find Emma and her abductors. He'd have to wait until an Apache was free of other duties to fly over here to begin a search pattern or he'd be shot out of the sky.

As he sat there in the cockpit of the helo, Khalid felt as if his whole world had turned black. Fear gripped him. Instinctively, Khalid felt this was Malik's work. The man was a sly enemy. And despite Jawid's best efforts to purge the valley of the Taliban, Malik had somehow managed to avoid detection.

He knew Khan and his soldiers were down in the valley. He picked up the radio and called the warlord. There was no signal. That wasn't unusual; among the sheer cliffs a radio signal could easily get lost. Khalid wiped his dry mouth with the back of his hand. His heart ached with fear for Emma. Malik would kill her. Worse, he would probably behead her. That was what the Taliban did to infidels. And especially if a woman soldier or pilot was captured, they were broadcasted as examples.

Khalid felt his heart explode with new grief and awareness. For so long, he had tried to tell himself he was not falling in love with Emma. That they were from very different worlds and countries. Yet, he *had* fallen in love with her! He closed his eyes, his hand pressed to his chest. There was such agony that he could barely breathe. He wanted Emma in his life. For the rest of his life. How could she be gone, ripped suddenly and unexpectedly from his life, from his heart?

Opening his eyes, Khalid felt a new emotion. It wasn't love. It was hatred. Despite only being half Afghan, the blood of the warrior was genetically as much a part of him as his Irish mother's side was. His eyes narrowed as he looked out over the green floor of the V-shaped rocky valley. Emma did not deserve this. None of it! She loved the Afghan people and these villagers loved her in return. She had made so many friends. True, loyal friends for life among them. She had done nothing wrong, and yet, Malik had captured her.

Getting up, Khalid cautioned himself to wait. He couldn't just take off and go find Emma. The infrared on an Apache could spot body heat miles away. It was their only chance to find her. Without hesitation, Khalid skidded down the ramp. The men had made short work of getting the rest of the boxes out of the hold of the cargo helo. His boots created a metallic echo as he left the ramp and stood in front of the men who had finished searching the slope.

One man, who had part of his arm missing, came forward and handed Khalid a green scarf. "This belonged to mem sahib," he told him. "We found it among the brambles near the base of the slope. There are footprints of five men. And we found where they hid their horses." He pointed toward the other side of the valley. "We can track them, Captain Shaheen. We have good daylight, half a day. Can we go after them?"

Khalid felt torn. The Afghan warrior in him wanted to leap upon a horse and lead these crafty men who knew how to track in even the worst of circumstances. Yet, as an officer in the U.S. Army, he had to wait for that Apache gunship to arrive. None was available for at least three hours. By then, Malik would escape. Holding up his hand, he told the man, "Hold on. I'll be right back. Mount up and get me a horse."

Khalid made a radio call to BJS 60 and told them what was going on. To his relief, Major Klein gave him permission to ride with Khan's men to start tracking Malik in hopes of finding Emma. She ordered him to take a satellite radio with him so they were in contact at all times. Klein understood there were no Apaches presently available and their only chance to find Emma was to do it the old-fashioned way: with men on horseback tracking their enemy.

Khalid pulled open his helmet bag. Inside was a curved dagger in a leather sheath. He removed it and set it on the seat. Glancing over, he imagined Emma sitting on the other seat. His heart contracted with such anguish that tears drove into his eyes. Khalid blinked them back, forced down all his emotions. He jammed all the extra cartridges for his .45 pistol into the leg pockets of his uniform. He found it comforting to strap on the dagger to the right side of his waist. This dagger had been in his father's family for eight hundred years. It had belonged to a caliph and had been a present to one of Khalid's relatives who was a powerful warlord in the region. Touching it, his fingers brushed the jewel-encrusted leather sheath. Khalid silently swore he would use it to cut Malik's throat.

Chapter 14

Fahran bit down hard on his lower lip. He crouched within a grayish cave that had poor light. For an hour, they'd ridden hard with their prisoner—the woman he and Benham had lured down the slope of Zor Barawul. Frightened, he watched as Lord Malik shoved the woman, Captain Emma Cantrell, off her feet. He hid his face, his back up against the cold, jutting rocks. Fahran felt no pain for himself, but anguish for the semi-conscious woman.

He saw Benham standing near the knot of

Taliban soldiers who encircled the woman. Her hands were tied in front of her and she was helpless against the jeering, cursing men. How could he have done this to Emma? How? Tears leaked into Fahran's eyes and he looked away as Malik lifted the toe of his boot and savagely kicked the woman in the ribs.

He heard Emma cry out. Suddenly, she went limp within the circle; dirt was smeared across her face and through her hair. Gulping and sobbing, Fahran stood up on tiptoe to see if she was dead. He bobbed his head from one side to another to see if she moved. Oh, why had he been talked into this by Lord Malik? Emma had always been nice to him and Benham. She'd brought both of them special gifts that no one else received. She'd even brought him the pair of fine leather shoes and the socks he now wore with pride.

Guiltily, Fahran gazed down at his shoes. They had been expensive, that he knew. To denote their worth, there was fine leather crafts-manship and colorful stripes on either side. Fahran had never had a pair of shoes in his life until Emma brought them for him. And how had he repaid her? Wiping his eyes, he crept closer. Was Emma dead? Had Lord Malik killed her with his boot? Gulping, Fahran wedged in between two soldiers.

Emma Cantrell lay unconscious within the circle of men, her face dirty and pale. Fahran thought surely she must be dead. His gaze shot to Malik who swaggered into the circle. The warlord's eyes were black with hatred. He kicked Emma again, this time in the shoulder. She moved like a rag doll, no sound issuing from her slack lips. Benham was grinning like the idiot he was. He liked hurting Emma.

What could he do? Fahran blinked back the tears, for he knew if any of these rugged, hard soldiers saw him cry, they would give him the boot, too.

"Leave her," Malik boomed. He looked around. "Come, let us eat in the other cave. They will never find us here." He grinned triumphantly.

The soldiers shouted a roar of approval. This cave was a very secret place and to get to it, one had to follow a series of tunnels. Their horses were tied up in a smaller, nearby cave. They would eat a hot meal, the smoke being carried down into another cave that no one could climb into.

Malik spied Fahran. "You!" he growled, pointing his finger at him. "Take care of this bitch when she wakes up."

One of the soldiers next to Fahran gave him a pistol from his belt.

Fahran gulped and nodded. "Y-yes, my lord," he whispered.

Suddenly, everyone was gone. Fahran could smell the wonderful scent of curry on the cool breeze moving silently through the series of caves. He stared down at Emma, who was motionless. Frightened that she was dead, Fahran dropped the pistol onto the dirt floor and knelt at her side after everyone had left.

Gently, he put his dirty hand on her shoulder. "Mem sahib Emma? Are you all right? Please wake up? Please," he choked in a whisper as he leaned near her ear, "don't be dead...."

The cave was cold. They always were. Fahran took his jacket, which Emma had brought him, and he carefully laid it across her shoulders and back to try and protect her from the draft. Hesitantly, he touched her cheek. She was so pale. Her freckles stood out in dark-brown spots across her ashen flesh. Terrible memories of his family dying a year ago slammed into him. He had leaned over his mother who was bleeding from the mouth, ears and nose after the bomb had exploded. She too had had her olive skin turn ashen just like Emma's. *Oh, Allah! Emma cannot be dead!* Why, oh why had he listened to Benham when he was given the order by Malik to lure either Emma or Kinah down the slope? Benham had swaggered, proud that he, of all people, had been chosen to initiate the trickery.

Malik had told Benham to take Fahran, too. Benham, of course, was in charge, Malik had assured the thirteen-year-old, patting him on the shoulder. Fahran hadn't wanted anything to do with the plan. Yet, he knew Benham would kill him if he didn't go along with it. On the way across the valley, Fahran had tried to find a way to detour Benham from the plan, to no avail. Benham had captured a baby goat and tied it in a thicket. He would jab it every once in a while with a sharp stick to get it to bleat. They'd hunkered down with the baby and watched Emma coming their way.

Two of Malik's best soldiers had then sneaked up and waited for Emma. When she'd gotten tangled in the thick brush, they'd attacked her. In seconds, she had been knocked unconscious. It had been easy to drag her to the horses tied below. One soldier mounted and the other hung her across his horse's withers. Benham leaped upon his horse and Fahran rode behind him, clinging for dear life as they thundered down a narrow trail that would lead them across the valley to their hidden cave complex.

Emma groaned. Pain made her open her eyes. At first, everything was blurry. Pain was radiating from her left shoulder. Her left hand felt numb and she couldn't feel her fingers. Her head throbbed. And so did her cheek and jaw. Blinking, she realized Fahran was kneeling next to her, his little face anxious.

"Mem sahib! You live!" He touched her jacketed shoulder.

It took long moments for Emma to realize what had happened—and where she was. Fahran jabbered on in Pashto, telling her everything. Her ears were still ringing, probably from the blow she'd taken earlier to the head. Fahran started to cry.

"I—I'm so sorry, mem sahib Emma. You did not deserve this. I—I couldn't do anything. I tried to get Benham to stop the plan. Oh! I thought you were dead after Lord Malik kicked you in the back."

Emma lay with her cheek against the fine, cool dust of the cave floor for nearly five minutes, trying to absorb what had happened. Fahran's tears rolled down his taut face making tracks through the dust on his cheeks. She tried to reach out with her left hand, but pain made her grunt. Her arm fell helplessly to the floor.

"Fahran," she croaked, "help me stand up. Can you do that?" Emma saw the pistol laying in the dirt about fifty feet away. She knew from Fahran that he was supposed to guard her. A mere ten-year-old. Hatred for Malik gave Emma the strength she needed. As she sat up, holding her left arm tight against her body, she closed her eyes until the dizziness passed.

Fahran anxiously circled her. "What are you

going to do, mem sahib?" He told her what Malik had done to her. That he'd kicked her twice.

Emma opened her eyes. She knew her left shoulder blade had been dislocated by Malik's kick. "Help me stand. I need to reset my shoulder blade."

Fahran gripped her right hand. Between them, Emma got to her feet. She staggered. Fahran threw his small arms upward and around her hips to steady her. It was enough. Emma heard voices wafting through the cave complex. She guessed the Taliban soldiers were not very close. The voices were muted. *Good.*

"Help me get to the wall," she ordered, her voice low with pain. Every time she took a faltering step, the agony made her groan. Gritting her teeth, she relied on Fahran's strength to get her to the wall of the cave.

Leaning against it, breathing hard, she felt

Fahran's hands continue to steady her. "I'm—okay," Emma told the boy. "Stand back."

Fahran backed away. He gave Emma a quizzical look. What was she going to do?

Emma sucked in a breath. *Oh, God, this is going to hurt....* She hurled her back against the cave wall as hard as she could. There was a *snap* and her shoulder blade seated back into its correct position. Emma blacked out from the overwhelming pain and fell, unconscious, to the floor.

Fahran cried out and raced forward. Emma was dead! What had she done to herself? She lay on her stomach, her arms flung away from her body. Dropping to his knees, he sobbed out her name and shook her shoulder, trying to awaken her.

Emma groaned. She felt Fahran's small hands gripping her flight suit near her right shoulder. The moment she groaned, he leaped way, frightened. The pain in her shoulder ebbed now as she pushed herself up into a sitting position. Fahran's eyes were huge. Tears glimmered in his dark eyes. "I'm okay," she rasped.

With a moan, Fahran walked toward her, unsure. "A-are you dead? Or are you alive?"

Emma forced a smile that was more like a grimace. "I'm alive, Fahran. I dislocated my left shoulder." She vaguely gestured toward the cave wall. "I threw myself into the wall to reset it. Do you understand?"

"N-no."

Emma felt stronger, more clear-headed. Her left shoulder ached, but nothing like before. She tested her left arm and lifted it a little. There was pain, but it was now manageable. Worriedly, Emma couldn't feel three of her fingers on her left hand. Had there been nerve damage when Malik kicked her unconscious? Had his boot severed those nerves? Fear struck her as she slowly opened and closed her left hand. If she couldn't get back sensation in those fingers, she would never be allowed to fly again.

"You must come with me," Fahran urged, coming over to where she sat. He whispered the words fiercely and kept looking toward the exit where the Taliban soldiers had left.

"Where? Where am I, Fahran? Can you help me get out of here?" She saw him screw up his small, thin face. He looked down a dark tunnel that lay opposite. Some grayish light came through it.

"You are on the other side of the valley opposite Zor Barawul," he told her. Anxiety raised his voice and he sounded reedy. "You must follow me, mem sahib Emma. I know another way out of here! But it is dangerous. And only small people can slide through the opening."

Emma nodded. "Am I small enough?" Her heart beat with hope. She heard the drifting voices of the soldiers. Would they come back and check on her? Emma knew Malik would kill her.

"Yes, yes, you are." Fahran held his small hands about an inch apart in front of her face. "It is late afternoon. We can wriggle like escaping rabbits away from Lord Malik." Anxiously, the boy looked at the opening. "They are eating and drinking now. There's a great celebration because you were captured."

Grimacing, Emma got to her feet. She gripped Fahran's slender shoulder. "Show me the way to get out of here. Can you take me out of these caves and get me clear of Malik and his men?"

"Yes, yes, I can." Fahran walked over to the pistol and then brought it back to Emma. "You keep this. I cannot kill anything."

Her heart broke over the boy's sudden, sagging face, tears in his eyes. Emma took the pistol and made sure there was a bullet in the chamber and the safety was off. "I understand," she told him gently. Patting his dusty hair, she added, "Let's go to Zor Barawul, Fahran. Take me home."

The sun slanted steeply on the western horizon when Malik heard the cry of a guard. It was the soldier standing at the mouth of the second cave. Malik had been crouched in front of the fire, eating a juicy, warm rabbit leg. The scent of curry and hot tea filled the small, warm cavern. Malik stood up, the leg of the roasted rabbit in his left hand.

"Lord Malik!" the soldier panted, running into the cave. "Riders! Lord Khan and his men! They're coming our way!"

"Mount up!" Malik roared. He took several more tearing bites from the rabbit and then threw it away. Turning, he said to Benham, "Get the American bitch. Bring her here to me."

"Yes, Lord Malik!" Benham pirouetted and raced for the smaller cave via a tunnel.

Everyone else quickly stored their meager utensils in rags and hurried down another tunnel to where all the horses were tethered. Malik scowled. It would be impossible for Khan to find this place. This cave complex had never been discovered. Touching the dagger at his waist and then his pistol next to it, Malik picked up his AK-47 and ran down the tunnel toward the saddled horses.

Benham gasped as he skidded to a halt in the other cave. Breathing hard, he looked around. Where was the American pilot? And Fahran? Suddenly scared, Benham wondered if she had overpowered Fahran and run. But where? Anxiously, Benham searched the entire cave. Nothing. There were no voices, no noises. No—anything. Suddenly afraid, Benham spun around and raced as fast as he could. Lord Malik needed to know his prisoner had escaped.

Malik had just grabbed the reins of his white stallion when Benham burst into the cave. His black-and-gray brows drew down. "Where's the American?" he roared at the approaching teenager.

"Gone!" Benham cried, sinking to his knees. All around him, riders and horses swirled. The tension was electric, dust raised by the horses suddenly whinnying and prancing around.

"What are you talking about?" Malik thundered as he mounted. He rode over to the cowering youth.

Benham choked out what he'd seen. "I-is there another way out of there, my lord?"

Scowling, Malik snarled, "Yes. It's a small, narrow passage." He glowered at the big, lumbering Benham. "You're too large to go in there to see if you can find them." He jerked his head around and barked orders above the din. A very small, wiry soldier came running forward.

"Siamak, go into the tunnel where the American was being kept prisoner. She's escaped into it. Find her. Kill her. Then, join us near Do Bandi. I'll see your horse is left here for you."

Nodding, Siamak bowed and took out his curved dagger from his belt. "As you wish, my lord." He turned and ran out of the cave.

Turning, Malik raised his hand and roared, "Follow me!" He jerked his stallion's reins and then trotted down another twisting, winding tunnel. Someone had lit a torch, the yellow and red flames flickering ahead of Malik.

Malik grinned savagely. He knew that this half-mile long tunnel, barely ten feet high, would lead them to a brush-covered opening that Khan knew nothing about. Within half an hour, they would be gone. Malik seriously doubted if Khan would even find this cave. It was all but impossible.

Gasping for breath, her shoulder burning, Emma crawled and wriggled through the blackness. Only Fahran's small shoes near her face kept her hopes up.

"A little more!" Fahran gasped.

Hope sprung up in her. It felt as though she'd wormed her way through the narrow, twisting tunnel forever. Every time she reached with her left hand to pull herself forward, the burning sensation deepened in her shoulder blade. She tried to use her right arm, but it was difficult. Her head throbbed and Emma wished mightily for some aspirin.

As they inched around a curve, Emma gasped. Light! She saw sunlight coming in through massive bushes that grew in front of the entrance. She saw Fahran's head bobbing up and down as he quickly scooted forward on his belly. Within three minutes, they were out of the tunnel and standing outside the thickets.

Holding her left arm against herself, Emma looked around. It was near sunset. The sky was a deepening blue as the rays of the sun shot across the tops of the peaks above them. Fahran dusted himself off the best he could.

Emma glanced down at her flight suit: she was dirty from top to bottom. She turned toward the small, narrow inlet. "Fahran, is there a trail down to the valley?"

"Yes," he said, suddenly smiling, relief in his face, "this way!"

Khalid rode with Jawid Khan, who had shown up with more men as they rode down through the valley. Khan's white stallion was a pure Arabian, small and powerful. Khalid's black gelding scrambled to keep up as they took a narrow, steep and rocky path up the side of a hill. Above them were caves. His terror over Emma being taken had tripled in the last two hours as they rode at high speed.

At the top of the hill, Khalid pulled his stallion to a skidding stop. His eyes were narrowed and he jabbed his finger to the left. Khalid squinted. He could see dust clouds rising far above them.

"What?" Khalid demanded, coming abreast of the panting white stallion.

Khan grinned. "Dust clouds indicate a large group of Taliban, brother. That is Malik! Let's go!" He spurred his stallion up the steep hill, pulling out his rifle from the sheath as he did so.

Khalid didn't question the man. Khan knew signs of Taliban better than anyone. His gelding was shiny with sweat, foam on his neck as he plunged up the hill on the heels of the white Arabian.

Khan gave a war cry of triumph as he breasted the hill. Khalid quickly saw why. There, no more than a mile away, in a slight meadow area, were twenty fleeing Taliban. And leading them on a white stallion was Malik himself.

"Do you see Emma?" he shouted to Khan, who was busy cocking his rifle.

Looking through his binoculars, Khan shook his head. "She's not among them. Once we get them, we'll find her location!" Khan whirled around, gesturing violently to his two hundred horsemen. For once, the odds were on his side. Normally, the Taliban outhorsed them and had more ammunition than they did. But not this time.

"Lord Khan!" Khalid shouted and pointed to the sky as two Apache helicopters hove into view. He pulled out his radio to direct the pilots to fire on the Taliban, "Malik is mine!"

Grinning wolfishly, Khan nodded. "As you will, brother. Let the Apache helicopters finish him off!"

Khalid knew he shouldn't feel happy about killing twenty people, but he did. Since Emma wasn't with them, he had the luxury of using the Apaches. As he called in the air strike, he wondered where she was. Had Malik hidden her in a cave? More than likely. Was she even alive?

Chapter 15

Emma was startled by two Apache helos flying overhead. They were firing off major expenditures of rockets. She heard the thuds, the explosions high up on the ridge above where they stood on the valley floor. Fahran clung to her, his head buried against her. Emma held him with her right arm, her left arm nearly useless. For about ten minutes, the combat helicopters circled like buzzards over an unseen prey. She couldn't see who or what they were targeting, but guessed it was Malik and his horsemen.

Grimly, Emma watched. She hoped the son of a bitch died.

"Come on," she urged Fahran. Looking up, she noted that the sun had set, but the well-used trail was easy to see. "We've got another mile before we reach the village," she told the boy.

Where was Khalid? Emma knew he'd be looking for her. They scrambled up the steep and rocky shrub-strewn slope. Breathing hard, slipping and sometimes falling, Emma thought she might be more mountain goat than human. Fahran, who was much lighter and smaller, climbed ahead. Sometimes, he would turn and hold out his small hand toward her. Emma's left shoulder ached badly and her left arm felt better if she didn't use it. She had to get to a doctor as soon as possible once she got back to the village.

As they huffed up the last, steep slope, Fahran cried out and pointed to the left. "Riders!"

Emma gasped and hunkered down on the

gravel slope, the sharp stones biting into her knees. About a mile away on another trail that led directly to the village, she saw a band of over two hundred riders at a hard gallop. In the lead was Jawid Khan. Her eyes narrowed. Yes! Khalid rode next to him! Her heart tumbled and for the first time, Emma allowed the suppressed emotions to surge up through her. Khalid! He'd gone out on horseback hunting for her. And he was safe. Gulping, Emma fought away the tears.

"Come on, we'll meet them at the village," she told the smiling Fahran, her voice hoarse with tears.

The last thing Khalid expected to see when he galloped into the village of Zor Barawul was Emma standing in the center of the village with bedraggled-looking Fahran in hand. He skidded his gelding to a halt and leaped out of the saddle, his booted feet hitting the ground at a run.

"Emma!" he called, his voice cracking with emotion. How pale she looked. Emma held her left arm against her body, her right hand protectively drawn across Fahran's thin shoulders.

"Khalid!" Emma didn't care who in the village saw them. She rushed forward after releasing Fahran. Emma extended her right hand toward him. Khalid's eyes filled with anguish and joy. As he approached, he gripped her hand and then closed the distance.

"You're alive," he whispered, leaning down and kissing her mouth tenderly.

Emma's world anchored only to Khalid's warm, cherishing mouth against hers. She moaned softly and leaned against his strong male body. He took all her weight and carefully held her, as if she were a priceless glass vase that might shatter at any moment. The warm moistness of his breath reminded Emma of life, instead of death. She could have died. She knew that. Emma loved Khalid with a fierceness that

swept through her as he took her mouth com-
mandingly a second time.

Breaking contact with her, Khalid looked
critically into Emma's softened and teary green
eyes. They were marred with pain. And relief.
And love—for him. Was that really possible?
Stunned, Khalid hadn't expected to see that.
Did Emma love him? Her eyes were shining
with joy—for him alone. Her lips trembled and
then she fought back the tears.

"Malik dislocated my left shoulder in the
cave," she whispered. She looked down at
Fahran. "He helped me escape, Khalid. He's the
real hero here. Fahran risked his life to show me
another way out of that cave complex."

Khalid tousled Fahran's dusty hair. "Thank
you, my brother."

Fahran looked shyly up at the pilot and managed an embarrassed shrug.

"There's a medevac flying in right now," he
told Emma, his fingers wrapping around her

right arm. Sweat and smudges of dirt covered her face. Even her red hair was dust-coated. "Can you walk? Or do you want me to carry you?"

Giving him a half laugh, because it hurt to move with the inflamed and injured shoulder, Emma said, "God, no. Just keep a steady hand on me, Khalid." Worried because three of her fingers were still numb, Emma wanted to see a doctor as soon as possible. The people of the village came out and offered help. Khalid thanked them and told them that Emma would be flown back to the base for medical treatment.

Near the edge of town, Kinah rushed over. She had concern on her face and her eyes were dark with worry. Emma assured her she would be okay after they carefully hugged one another.

"Malik's dead," Khalid told his sister with grim satisfaction. "The two Apaches came in and destroyed his entire army. There's not much left of any of them." He had wanted to race down that slope and meet Malik on the field of battle. Instead, Khalid had called in the combat mission over his portable radio. The two Apache helicopters had loosed an arsenal of ammunition that had killed every Taliban rider. Including Malik.

Emma closed her eyes for a moment. Then, she looked down at Fahran, who refused to leave her side. "Benham was with Malik?" she asked the child.

"Yes, he was, mem sahib."

Nodding, Emma told Khalid what had happened. She saw the medevac flying over the mountain crest and heading directly for the landing zone just outside the village. Khalid gently placed his arm around Emma for just a moment, his embrace butterfly-light.

"We'll get you to Bagram. I know all the doctors there. We'll get you to an orthopedic and neurology specialist, Emma. He'll make you well." He bored a look into her fatigued eyes. All he wanted to do was kiss her senseless and hold her tightly against him and protect her from a world gone mad. But he could do none of those things right now. Khalid swallowed his frustration. He had to be patient. Emma was worried about her numbed fingers. All he could do was be at her side.

Kinah came forward and grasped Fahran's hand as the medevac landed, the blades whirling and kicking up dust clouds. "I'll take care of him," she called to them. "Be well, Emma. Brother, let me know how she is?"

Khalid nodded. Kinah had a military radio that was always on her person. Plus, the A-team that was stationed at the village could always be contacted to let her know the latest news. "I will, my sister."

Once the medevac had shut down, Khalid led Emma to the open door. Welcoming hands ushered her into the helo. As Khalid climbed in and made sure Emma was being taken care of, a bit of relief sank into him. Khalid had terrible memories of finding Najela dead. He didn't think he could go through the same thing again.

"I can't believe it," Emma told Khalid as she walked into his home near Kabul. "Thirty days leave." Her left arm was in a sling and she had been given pain medication for her dislocated shoulder.

Khalid opened the door. "I can. Come, we'll get you into your suite and you can take a long, hot bath." The sky was dark, with sparkling stars, the wind hot off the desert. Inside, air conditioning welcomed them. He shut the door. Rasa, his housekeeper had been called earlier, and she stood attentively at the end of the hall near the living room.

In Pashto, Khalid asked Rasa to escort Emma to her suite. He leaned over and pressed a kiss to her hair. "If you want to go directly to bed, do so. I will be up for a while." He motioned toward the kitchen. He'd eaten little in the last twenty-four hours.

Emma nodded as she noticed the darkness beneath Khalid's eyes. "Okay," she whispered. "I'm not hungry, just dirty and tired. The bath sounds perfect. Good night." After hours in the medical facility at Bagram, being poked, prodded and X-rayed, Emma felt so fatigued that her feet moved like chunks of concrete across the tiled floor. She'd had serious bruising on her cheek and ribs, but nothing was broken, thank goodness. Bath and bed sounded wonderful. She smiled at the housekeeper, and the woman nodded and smiled shyly in return.

"Only good dreams," Khalid said, giving Emma a raw look of love.

"Good dreams," she murmured. Emma looked over her shoulder to see Khalid striding silently into the kitchen. What she wanted was to be with him. To bathe, get her hair washed and slip into Khalid's bed and be held in the loving protection of his arms. It was another dream….

Swallowing, Emma understood that it couldn't be. At least, not right now. The doctor at Bagram said she'd suffered nerve damage to the three fingers of her left hand. Worse, he had no idea if she would get feeling back in them or not. And, the final blow to Emma was that she could not fly until—or if—she got full use of her fingers back. Emma felt as though the world had crashed in on her. She reminded herself she'd get out of the dirty flight suit, clean up and, she hoped, sleep deeply. Tomorrow morning, she would be in a better frame of mind.

Emma sat up screaming. The shout that erupted from within her startled her awake. Breathing raggedly, she shakily touched her perspiring face. Even with her eyes open, the light from the moon coming in the window, she could still see the hatred for her in Malik's eyes. That had been seconds before he'd kicked her in the ribs and knocked her unconscious.

"God," she muttered, throwing off the sheet and planting her bare feet on the cool tile floor. The slight movement of air conspired to help her focus on the present, not the past. Emma moved her left arm tentatively. She was on pain medication and now it moved easily and without any problem. Getting up, she found the lavender silk robe at the bottom of her queen-sized bed. As she pulled it on, Emma wanted to escape the room—and Malik's leering face. Maybe a hot cup of tea would help.

Heart pounding, Emma made her way through the darkened halls to the living room. This was her favorite place in Khalid's home. There were leather couches strewn with colorful pillows and a beautiful Persian rug lay between the two massive couches. She halted and gasped. "Khalid!"

"Emma." Khalid swallowed his shock at seeing her and quickly stood up. He'd been leaning against some pillows propped up against one of the massive sofas. Dressed in a dark-blue cotton robe, he stared at her in confusion as she anchored at the door.

He saw the dark circles beneath Emma's eyes even as the moonlight sprawled through the massive picture window. Her flesh gleamed. It was then that it hit him: she'd had a nightmare. More than likely a reaction to her trauma. "Please," Khalid whispered, "come in. I can leave if you like?" He had no desire to make her feel trapped. The wildness in her dark-green eyes haunted him. Khalid saw the fear etched in them. Praying it was not fear of him, he lifted his hand and opened it to her.

"I—uh…no, stay." Helplessly, Emma said in a shaky voice, "I had a nightmare about Malik just before he kicked me. I woke up screaming. Did I wake you up, too?"

Khalid watched her with such gentleness in his eyes. "No. I've been up for a while." He motioned to the book near the pillows. "I was reading and hoping to get tired enough to go to sleep."

Emma saw how very old the book was. The leather was frayed and worn. Somehow, just talking with Khalid was helping calm her down. "I wish I could read a book and feel safe…feel…okay," Emma gulped. Clinging to Khalid's dark gaze, all she wanted to do was run to him. As if reading her mind, he walked toward her, his arms opening, silently asking her to come to him. Emma didn't shy away from her raw feelings for Khalid.

Moving into his arms and feeling his strength and tenderness, her face pressed to his neck and jaw, Emma released a long, trembling sigh.

"You're safe with me, beloved," Khalid rasped near her ear. Tendrils of her unbound hair tickled his chin and lips. Inhaling her feminine scent, he felt Emma sag completely against him, her arms sliding around his waist. He closed his eyes and savored her trust of him. Without thinking, he pressed small kisses upon her mussed, clean hair. "It's going to be all right," he breathed against her ear. "We have one another, Emma. The world might unhinge, but we love one another. And with love, we can get through anything. Together."

Tears beaded along Emma's lashes. "I feel so weak, Khalid. So scared. My whole life is upended. What if I don't get feeling back into my fingers? My God, I can't fly. The army won't allow it. Where will I go? What will I do? All I've known is the army and flying."

Khalid absorbed her sob. Emma's fingers dug into his robe and chest. "Let it out, Emma. I'm here…I'll hold you against the storms."

Emma had never felt so safe or so loved as in that moment. There was something so exotic and ancient about Khalid. He was a warrior at heart. A man who could wear his heart on his sleeve without apology. And he knew when to be tender and sensitive. She had never found all these qualities in one man before. She had in Khalid. As hot tears spilled out of her eyes and streaked down her cheeks, Emma trusted Khalid with her life. She cried out her fear of having no future as a pilot, of having her world suddenly turned upside down and not knowing where she was going to land. Only the safety, the stability of Khalid's strong arms holding her tightly against him was real.

Eventually, Emma's sobs ceased. She hiccuped a few times. Khalid gently moved her toward the sofa and they sat down together. She eased back into his arms and he simply held her. With her head resting against his shoulder, her silky hair against his jaw, Khalid closed his eyes. He could feel Emma's heart pounding against his chest. Felt the touch of her hand against his damp robe. He tenderly slid his fingers through her mussed hair. This was the first time Khalid had explored her and it made his heart swell fiercely with love for Emma. He felt her nestle her cheek more deeply against the crook of his shoulder. The fast beat of her heart was slowing now.

"Crying is a good thing," he told her. "I remember when I was a little boy and my pet canary died, I cried for days afterward. He was my friend and at seven years old I didn't understand that things could die. My parents encouraged my tears and they held me. I was lucky to have their understanding. I learned about death and that I could be held with love in the aftermath."

Just hearing Khalid tell his story soothed Emma's fractious state. She sat up and wiped her cheeks free of the spent tears. "I feel like I'm dying, Khalid." Emma held up her left hand and looked at it. "I have this horrible gut feeling that I'm not going to get rid of the numbness in my fingers. That the army will ask me to give up my commission." Emma searched his eyes. "What will I do then?" The question was hard to ask, but she felt as if Khalid saw into her soul and never judged her.

Reaching up, he pushed a few errant tendrils of hair away from her face. "Beautiful Emma, you are young. You have your whole life ahead of you. Sometimes, we have one door shut in our face. But as soon as that happens, another will open. That is the way it is."

Emma nodded, barely able to keep from staring down at her hand. "My family is a military one, Khalid. Most of us serve our country. Casey didn't, but that's okay, too. She's my younger sister." Dragging in a deep breath, Emma expended it and frowned. "The army won't wait long to see if I can fly again. If I can't, they'll release me. What good to them is a pilot who can't fly?"

Touching her left hand, Khalid stroked each of

her long, artistic fingers. "Listen to me, Emma. I have had many dreams for you—and me." He snagged her glance and smiled unsurely. "I have dreamed of asking you to marry me. To be my partner. I have dreamed of us flying books and school materials all along the border of my country—together." He held her left hand. "The military might not let you fly, but there is nothing to say you can't fly a commercial helicopter. You know, I own a fleet of them. I have three. I have used them for years to help Kinah fulfill our destiny with our Afghan brothers and sisters. You know me as flying for the military, but my life is much broader and deeper than that."

Amazed, Emma stared at him. Her heart pounded. Khalid wanted to marry her! She vaguely heard the rest of his words, her gaze locked with his. There was such tenderness in his eyes for her. Real love. Not some passing infatuation, but love. Emma knew the difference. She twined her fingers between Khalid's. "From the moment I met you, Khalid, I fought my attraction to you. At first, I thought you were just like Brody Parker. But over time, I knew that wasn't so. Every time we kissed, I wanted so much more from you. I wanted to know everything about you. How you grew up. What held your interest. What experiences you went through to make you the man who is sitting here with me now."

Lifting his hand, Khalid cupped her cheek. "And I fought loving you, Emma. After Malik murdered Najela, I felt as if my whole life was over. I couldn't conceive of ever loving another woman." He grazed her cheek. "Until I met you. Then, everything changed for me, Emma." Touching the area of his heart, Khalid whispered unsteadily, "I felt as if my life were given back. A second chance. And once I realized I loved you with a fierceness to match the breadth of my life, I wondered if you loved me.

You know in the military we can't show our affection with one another. It's not allowed."

Emma nodded. "I know...and I wanted so badly to tell you, Khalid, but I was scared. We're from different countries. Different worlds. I was worried how our parents would get along. I was worried about a lot of things, so it stopped me from telling you how I really felt." Emma closed her eyes as his fingers trailed down her cheek to trace the length of her slender neck. Khalid had to know the truth. "Where would we live? What kind of life would be expected of me by you? I had so many questions and no answers."

Khalid dropped his hand and held on to her searching gaze fraught with worry. "My mother is Irish. My father is Afghan. I was raised in a home where nothing but love and respect ruled. My father, whom I know you will love, is a man of great heart. He respects everyone. Their beliefs. Their individualism. My mother is tolerant of all peoples. She sees only their hearts and their dreams."

"Your parents are like mine in that way," Emma said.

Khalid managed an unsteady smile. "When one is raised in such an environment, Emma, how can one have problems with any other? I believe you have the right to ask those questions, but you must base the answer on your experiences with me. I can't believe that your family is prejudiced against anyone from a foreign country. You show a tolerance and respect similar to mine, so I know your family is heart-centered too. It's not the color of a person's skin or their particular beliefs that really matters."

"It's the only way I want to see the world, too. My parents taught us the real measure of a person was their humanity to others," Emma whispered.

Khalid tapped his heart with his hand. "Yes. The only question I ever have of anyone is whether they are coming from their heart. You come from your heart, beloved, just as I do. Is it not possible that two people who come from the heart can love and marry? That their families would also be celebrating such a union? When you marry for love and come into that sacred union with only love, then the best of all worlds has been born."

Emma saw how her doubts had no merit whatsoever. Khalid's voice was low with feeling. The more she knew the man, the more deeply she fell in love with him. Khalid was complex, with so many layers, and yet, he had a global perspective she didn't see as often in others. And that drew her powerfully to him. "You're right," Emma admitted quietly, brushing her fingers across his hand.

"Love moves mountains," Khalid told her. "No one can be untouched by love. I have dedicated my life, Emma, to doing things from my heart for others. Yes, I am rich monetarily, but

I prefer the richness that comes from the heart. It's not something money can buy. That is why it's so important to help my people here in Afghanistan. Kinah is the same. She sees our money as simply a way to a means. One that will lift our people, one child at a time, to be educated. Because getting an education will lift our nation out of the past and bring it into the present."

Emma saw the fervency in Khalid's narrow eyes. And she heard it in his voice. "You're a family of dreamers who put your vision into reality."

Smiling faintly, Khalid took her hand and pressed a soft kiss to the back of it. "I like that. Yes, that's true, beloved. Right now," he whispered, sitting up and framing her face, "all I want is you at my side, Emma. I want you as my partner for life. I cherish your ideas, how you see the world and how you see me. I want to fulfill your dreams, too. What is a life lived alone? It is empty and hungry. I want my life entwined with yours, Emma. Will you marry me?"

How could she say no? Khalid's words fell gently across her heart in such a way that Emma could not see her life without his larger-than-life presence in it. "Yes, I will marry you, Khalid. I'm not sure where our lives will lead, but it's going to be an adventure."

Leaning forward, he brushed her lips, parting them. "Beloved, no matter what we do, we will allow our hearts to lead the way...."

Chapter 16

Khalid picked Emma up and cradled her in his arms. She kissed his cheek and inhaled his dizzying male scent as she wrapped her arms around his broad shoulders. There was joy in his eyes, a fierce love for her that stole her breath. This man, who bridged two major religions, was living proof that east could meet west from the heart. Khalid was unique and Emma sighed as she rested her brow against his cheek. Her mother, Alyssa, had always said that whomever she married had to be more than just

a man. She had been right: Khalid was arche-
typal in the best of ways. Having been born and
lived in such a loving home where the Christian
and the Muslim religions were joined, he'd absorbed the best from both. And now, she was
going to live with this man who held the hope
of the world in his heart.

Emma smiled faintly as Khalid nudged the
door to his master bathroom open with his
toe. "Ah…water. I like where this is going,
Khalid…"

He gently placed her on the thick blue Persian
rug in front of a huge glass-enclosed double
shower. "Care to join me?"

Grinning, Emma watched as he stepped into
the blue-and-white tiled shower and turned on
the water. The multiple shower heads released
warm water that fell like soft raindrops. "Just
try and stop me."

Khalid smiled in response, then felt the temperature of the water. "Just right. Are you ready, beloved?"

Without hesitation, Emma slid the lavender robe off. She wore only a silky tank top and shorts that fell midway on her thighs. "I am. You?" She gave him a challenging smile.

Khalid had no shyness about removing his blue robe. He was completely naked beneath. If Emma was disappointed in him, her large, beautiful green eyes did not reflect that. As her gaze moved from his throat, down across his darkly haired chest to his flat stomach to his narrow hips, he saw her cheeks turn pink and those copper freckles darkened. Reaching out, he settled his hands lightly on her shoulders.

"Do I pass your inspection?"

His teasing made her laugh. A sudden, happy giddiness surged through Emma as she looked up into his glinting, narrowed gaze. "Oh, yes, you do." She saw how pleased Khalid was, and maybe, a bit relieved. After all, he was a flesh-

and-blood man and Emma knew he was probably worried she might not be pleased with his body. She felt him move the thin silk from her shoulders. Her skin flushed and then prickled pleasantly as he coaxed the material off her torso and exposed her breasts. In a moment, Khalid had removed the soft material and set it on a nearby shelf. His gaze moved hungrily across her body. She felt his desire even though he hadn't made a move to touch her. Her breasts tightened and the nipples hardened beneath his intense look.

Pushing the silky pajama pants off, Emma let them pool around her feet. She smiled and moved into the warm streams of water that issued from opposite walls within the huge shower. Gripping his hand, she said, "Come on in. The water's fine."

In moments, Khalid had closed the shower door, and the steam began to gather, moving in fine, thin ripples around them. Emma moved boldly into Khalid's arms. She wanted him and wasn't going to be coy about it. To her delight, his very male mouth curved over her brazen move. As soon as she slid her wet body up against his, his arms circled her. Leaning up, she claimed his smiling mouth. Emma unleashed all the hunger from the last months against Khalid. His mouth was strong, giving and taking against her own. As his tongue moved across her lower lip, she felt his hand slide teasingly down her spine. His fingers splayed and outlined each of her vertebrae, the water intensifying his burning touch. Khalid drew her powerfully against him and Emma gasped. She felt him smile and returned it. The water was like another set of her lover's hands as it curved and curled around her face, wetting her hair, the strands thickening and lying in fine sheets across her shoulders.

Khalid's mouth tore from hers and he trailed hot, hungry kisses from her jaw down the graceful line of her neck to her shoulders. With her left shoulder, he was tender and careful. Her skin sizzled with pleasure and danced with each slight brush of his exploring mouth. As Khalid eased her back, his hand splayed out against her spine to hold her steady, their hips melted into one another. His kisses sought and found each of her taut breasts. Emma sighed and gripped his tense arms that held her captive.

He tenderly mouthed each of her nipples, making her moan. The water sluicing across her face, down her shoulders and trickling in and around her breasts only increased her pleasure. Each kiss along the curve of each breast heightened Emma's need of him. Khalid's masculine power was nearly overwhelming. She felt him trembling and Emma intuitively understood he was holding back his fierce love for her. Because of her injured shoulder, she knew he was being gentle so that he wouldn't create more injury for her.

As Khalid brought her back against him, the water spilled over them, the heat and steam curling around them like the fingers of a thousand other tantalizing hands. He slid his hands down, down, down until he cupped her hips. And then Khalid lifted her against him. Her arms slid around his shoulders as he gently settled her against him. Inch by inch, he slowly lowered her down upon himself.

A raw, guttural sound of pleasure rose in Emma's throat. She threw her head back, her body melted hotly against Khalid's as she brought him within her throbbing core. The moment was powerful, the water running around them, fusing them even more wonderfully to one another. Emma leaned her head downward, found his mouth and kissed him hard. She didn't want him treating her like some fragile glass that might break. After all, it was only her shoulder. Emma felt him smiling beneath her mouth. In moments, Khalid was moving her, holding her and kissing her hungrily in return.

The steam swirled around them. The silken water fused and inspired them. Emma gripped Khalid's broad, powerful shoulders, suddenly tensing as the heat of her body burst open and flowed in a tidal rhythm. A groan of complete pleasure tore from her wet lips. She felt Khalid tense, a growl from deep within him rolling upward. The sound was like thunder, shared and absorbed between them.

Closing her eyes, taut as a bow against Khalid, Emma surrendered all her love into this man who held her in his arms. For long, golden moments, only he existed—a part of her, a part of her pounding heart rhythm in tune with his. She thought she'd known love before, but she really hadn't. The love that Khalid had shared with her, the respect, the joy was rare. And beautiful. And fulfilling.

As water coursed down her head, the strands of her red hair clinging to her wet face, she leaned over, framed Khalid's face and kissed him. Nothing had ever been as wonderful as this moment for Emma. She understood now what Khalid had said earlier about living from the heart. It was effortless and joyful. As their mouths cherished one another, took and gave, Emma knew this man was greater than most. Her spirit had seen his. She truly saw Khalid's heart and his love for her. And searching his soft blue eyes, Emma knew he looked into her soul with nothing but love. Together, they could do a lot in their own unique ways to help the world. What else was there but love? In her dizzied mind, her thoughts disjointed, Emma was ready to accept whatever life would hand her. After all, she had a man who loved her with a fierceness that took her breath away. All else would fall into some kind of order after that.

"I'm really sorry," Nike told Emma as they stood outside the HQ of the BJS 60 squadron. "I know Rachel would be here to support you today, but she's off on a mission."

"Don't be," Emma told her best friend. She smiled a little. On her left hand was an emerald ring that Khalid had given her a month ago. Rachel, her cousin, had wanted to be with her when she found out the army's decision, but a sudden fire fight along the border had broken out and all available women pilots were called to the Apache gunships to go help turn the tide.

Nike grimaced. The July sun was hot overhead, the nonstop sounds of helicopters landing and taking off nearby permeating the vibrating air. "You got feeling back in one finger, but not the other two. I don't know why the army refuses to let you fly. This is so stupid."

"Let it go," Emma counseled gently. "The army says a pilot has to have feeling in all ten fingers. Not eight. I'll be okay."

"I won't be," Nike griped. Upset, she jammed her hands on her hips. "The army should give you more than four weeks to heal up! Who's to say you won't get feeling back in those fingers two or three months down the road?"

"What are they going to do with a pilot who can't fly?" Emma asked. "Major Klein was very sorry she had to give me their decision. She said if it had been up to her, I'd still be with BJS 60."

"I know. Everyone in HQ knew when the decision by the army higher-ups had come down. Major Klein was in a really ugly mood for a couple of hours after that. That's how we all knew they'd decided against you staying. You seem to be at peace about this," Nike said. "Khalid's influence?"

"In part, yes." Emma put on her aviator sunglasses and settled the black BJS baseball cap on her head. "My family is fine with what has happened. Khalid and I have a plan. I'll now be a part of his family nonprofit charitable organization. I'll be allowed to fly commercial helicopters that he and his family own. And really, it's a good thing because I can fly into the safe villages with resupplies and the army won't have to do it." She grinned and began to walk with Nike toward the tent area. Emma would pick up the last of her clothes and other personal items from the tent she'd lived in for over a year, and then be escorted off base. For a new life. A new adventure. And with a man she loved and who loved her with a fierceness that made Emma feel as if she were floating on a cloud of nonstop joy.

"When it's all said and done," Nike told her, brightening a little, "you'll be allowed back on base because Khalid is assigned here."

"Yes, I will." Emma gave her an evil grin. "Down, but not out, Nike. I'm going to move my stuff into his home in Kabul. A week from now Khalid gets thirty days of leave from the army and we're going to fly home to San Francisco to be married. My entire family, uncles included, are coming. Even Rachel, my cousin, is being given leave to attend, thanks to Major Klein. She knows how much it means to my family to be there for our wedding."

"That's great. I wish I could be there, too."

"So do I. I was surprised Major Klein let Rachel go. This is our heavy season for Apache demands and we're now a pilot short because I had to resign my commission."

"I think Major Klein is a good C.O. I know she didn't want you to resign, but she can't buck army regs as much as she might have wanted to. You and Rachel will be back a month from now," Nike said, gloating. "And we'll just pick up where we left off, girlfriend." She threw her arm around Emma's shoulders and gave her a quick squeeze.

"We will," Emma promised her, voice thickening with tears. Nike was an incredible friend, someone she never wanted to lose touch with. Today, her life would change forever. It was a bittersweet moment for Emma. She'd been the casualty of this war in one way. In another way, this war had brought her the man she would love forever. And, she would have her cousin Rachel here with her. If she had learned anything, Emma had learned a long time ago that the only thing she could count on was change.

Emma opened up her tent. Nike followed and in quick order they had her personal belongings in the duffel bag. Her shoulder had healed up completely in the past month and it was easy enough to carry it over her right shoulder. Nike walked with her in the hot sunlight. The smell of aviation fuel, dust and the noise of trucks coming and going was a constant.

Emma was glad to be going home. Her family was in high gear to give them a July wedding at Golden Gate State Park near San Francisco's Golden Gate bridge. And San Francisco was one of Khalid's favorite cities in the world. Yes, Emma thought, it would be a whirlwind month filled with overflowing happiness for her entire family. But especially for her and for Khalid who loved her tenderly every night before they slept in one another's arms. She was excited to have the Cantrells and the Trayherns embrace Khalid and his family who would also be there for the wedding. They were a global family in so many ways already. Now, east was marrying west. She liked being a forerunner. And she loved Khalid, a man who had one foot in western civilization and the other firmly rooted in his beloved Afghanistan. She would love this fierce global warrior forever.

* * * * *

Mills & Boon® Online

Discover more romance at
www.millsandboon.co.uk

- **FREE** online reads
- **Books** up to one month before shops
- **Browse our books** before you buy

...and much more!

For exclusive competitions and instant updates:

 Like us on **facebook.com/romancehq**

 Follow us on **twitter.com/millsandboonuk**

Join us on **community.millsandboon.co.uk**

Visit us Online Sign up for our FREE eNewsletter at
www.millsandboon.co.uk